WRONG DOCTOR JOHN

At first dismayed when she is transferred to the unattractive Eye Clinic attached to Sydney's Southern Cross Hospital, Nurse Emma Brown soon finds how mistaken her opinion has been. Is she equally mistaken about young Doctor John Harding?

WRONG DOCTOR JOHN

BY
KATE STARR

MILLS & BOON LIMITED
London · Sydney · Toronto

First published in Great Britain 1966
by Mills & Boon Limited, 15–16 Brook's Mews,
London W1A 1DR

This edition 1983
© Kate Starr 1966

Australian copyright 1983
Philippine copyright 1983

ISBN 0 263 74381 0

Set in 10 on 11½ pt Linotron Times
03/0883

Photoset by Rowland Phototypesetting Ltd
Bury St Edmunds, Suffolk
Made and printed in Great Britain by
Richard Clay (The Chaucer Press) Ltd
Bungay, Suffolk

CHAPTER ONE

IT was a postcard sort of morning, a fresh, bright morning that brings wholeness and sanity flooding reassuringly back to a slightly threadbare, rather crazy world. Emma, feeling slightly threadbare and rather crazy herself after her worst Night so far in her row of Nights—old Beniston trying to saw down the legs of his cot because he said it was too high to climb into had been the last straw—paused a moment to let the sweet calm and gentle promise of the new day soak into her, just as the dew from the shrubs she was absentmindedly not avoiding was soaking into her starched skirts.

How fortunate, she was thinking abstractedly, that the Southern Star Hospital, for all its immediacy to Sydney, was no asphalt jungle as one might have expected when underground train tracks ran beneath and traffic boomed by the door.

Instead—and Emma inwardly bowed to some far-sighted founder—the lawns (and their soaking shrubs) made you forget the outside world. The freesias, the flaunting poppies and the thicket of graceful Norfolk Island pines made the city hospital almost a garden place.

That is, of course, if you excluded the Eyesore.

You could let your glance rove as far as the soaring Norfolks, but no farther. Behind the thicket of leaves, then farther down the hill, finally facing the next busy city street, showing slightly above the tall trees, desolately, dingily, discouragingly and unbelievably drably

5

stood the Eye Clinic. Hard to believe that it, too, was part of Southern Star.

Emma, like all the others, had not believed for quite a while that EC *was* as much Southern Star as the hospital itself.

'Oh, yes, it is,' a senior nurse, given the job of conducting around the current intake—with Emma in it—had breezily assented. 'What's more, it's the only Australian hospital devoted entirely to eye cases. Don't let its squalor deceive you, pros; only on the outside is Eye Clinic an eyesore.'

When they all politely applauded her wit she had added seriously, 'And I don't mean it's any better inside either, I'm talking in terms of what gets done.'

'It's ugly-old,' Lorraine had pointed out resentfully. 'Our Southern Star is lovely-old.'

'It was a big boarding house in the nineties,' Senior Nurse recited. 'Robert Louis Stevenson stayed there . . . Cobb and Co. coaches called.'

'It's still ugly,' Lorraine had said distastefully under her breath.

'Southern Star considered itself lucky to obtain the building when its eye clinic grew as tremendously as it did,' continued Senior Nurse. 'A hat factory was after it.'

'Pity they didn't succeed,' said Lorraine, but still, being a wise pro, under her breath.

When Senior Nurse had gone, though, she had re-named Southern Star's Eye Clinic the Eyesore, and the others, and Emma, had agreed. Fortunately it was so far away, three hundred yards at least, that it was easy not to include it whenever you showed your friends the particular institute of healing where you were learning to heal. In fact, in the two and a half years that had gone by since Emma's batch had first decried the Eye Clinic the girls had got into the habit of ignoring it altogether, of never looking farther than the thicket of splendid pines. If occasionally they did by accident, they crossed their fingers, looked around for wood to touch, then assured each other that once you went down the hill you never returned.

How awful, Emma thought now, approving everything about Southern Star and nothing about Eyesore, if one was transferred there, though, of course, that could not happen to a midway like she was. Only the experienced went there. And, Emma giggled uncaringly, never returned.

Her drenched skirts were now flapping uncomfortably against her legs, even in her abstraction she felt the wet limpness. She had been an idiot to walk between the shrubs. Yet it had been heavenly to feel coolness after heat, and that temperature of old Beniston's following his crazy sawing bout had been far too high; it even had raised Emma's own temperature in alarm. Emma stopped short suddenly. *Did* I put the saw back?

For a moment she stood frowning in the direction of the Eye Clinic—Eyesore was always good for a frown—then sighed and hunched her shoulders. I won't sleep till I make sure, she knew resignedly, so back I go again.

She ran across the grass, glad of the very early hour, which meant there would be no raised brows at her swishing skirts and general dampness, for dampness hadn't mattered when you had meant within ten minutes to be snug in bed. Now it would matter, that is if you had the foul luck to run into someone, but that, Emma thought, was improbable at under five a.m. yet past four, which was usually a deserted, emptyish hour.

She was lucky. She managed to check the saw without even a patient or a nurse noticing her, and certainly no sister did, and running out again, she shook off her cap as she dodged between the shrubs, letting the dew shower her bright red hair as well as her skirts, freed properly this time. No saws or temperatures to fret her, young again, uncaring, part of the postcard morning . . .

And from a window on the top floor of Southern Star a man looked down.

It was two days later that Staff Sister Stelling, having checked and re-checked . . . 'Be sure, Sister,' she had been instructed, 'to get the *right* one. A hospital of this size must have its load of redheads' . . . sent for Emma.

If it had been anyone but Mr John Harding, Sister Stelling would have refused to check; if the loftiness of the inquirer's position had demanded that she comply she would have seen to it privately that what was asked she deliberately did not find; but Mr John Harding was different. She had worked with him at the Eye Clinic. Though on principle she disapproved of doctors selecting a nurse, disapproved heartily, when it was Mr John Harding everything was different, and now she looked up without rancour at Emma Brown and said, 'Nurse, you are transferred.'

Children's, hoped Emma, who had had a rip-roaring time last go in Brats, or I wouldn't mind a session at Outpatients again, or Casualty, or—

'Yes, Sister?'

'EC.'

'The Eyesore?' gasped Emma.

'I beg your pardon?'

'The Eye—the Eye Clinic?'

'Yes, EC—the Eye Clinic. That's what I said.'

'But—it's a long way off.'

'It is precisely two hundred and ninety-five yards.'

'Mid-ways . . . I mean juniors, in-betweens, under-grads, my stage don't go there.'

'Nurse, are you trying to tell me what to do?'

'Oh, no, Sister.'

'It sounded very much like it. You will begin duty there tomorrow, then.'

'But—well—'

'Yes, Nurse?'

'Can I move my things down there in time? I mean—'

'Don't be absurd. You'll still live here, of course, there's no accommodation at EC.' No, thought Sister Stelling, no accommodation, no convenience, not even ordinary, decent working conditions, not anything at all—except dedicated, hard work.

'I—' mumbled Emma.

'That will be all, Nurse. Except—' Suddenly Sister Stelling wanted very much to know *how* all this had come about, *why* it had happened.

'Yes, Sister?'

'Have you met Mr Harding?' Sister asked carefully.

'Who? Oh, no.'

'I see.' Sister didn't see, but she still felt very much that she would like to, so she persisted.

'You've been on Nights,' she probed.

'Yes, Sister.'

Then that would be it, thought Sister Stelling shrewdly. John Harding would be just back from EC after a difficult night, the child would be running across the lawn, as undoubtedly by those slim legs she often, if secretly, ran, and her red hair, her flag-bright hair—

'You'd have your cap off.' She said it more to herself than to Emma.

Emma looked puzzled, thought back, then recalled. 'Well, I suddenly remembered Beniston and his wretched temperature after all that sawing. Not that he could get through iron, Sister, but the silly old man tried. It was really the hospital carpenter's fault, he shouldn't have left the tools where Beniston could find them. I'm afraid,' Emma faltered, 'the iron legs are badly scratched.'

Sister Stelling thought wearily that Nurse surely must know what she was talking about, for she, Sister, certainly didn't. She thought at the same time how that red head and flying figure would have arrested Mr John Harding's attention; colour, where everything where he worked was without colour, where frequently he knew there could be no more colour; dancing speed, where, because of a clouded world, feet came fumblingly, clumsily, painfully slow.

Yes, she could understand . . .

But Emma did not understand.

'Am I being punished, Sister Stelling?' she said pathetically.

'Punished?'

'To be sent to the Eyesore—I mean to EC?'

'A punishment? Our Eye Clinic?' There was such withering scorn in Sister Stelling's face that Emma felt smaller still than her smallness in her flat ward shoes.

'I—I'm sorry, Sister.'

The Sister brooded a moment on things she could have said, things she wanted to, but, remembering John Harding, instead she dismissed briskly, 'Tomorrow then. EC.'

'Thank you, Sister. EC.'

But out in the corridor Emma looked down on the building beyond the Norfolk pines, the building with every inconvenience a building should not have, looked at the drab gaol grey of it, the cavern-like door to it, the Abandon Hope look of it, and sighed, 'Eyesore' instead.

CHAPTER TWO

THE gang did nothing to restore once more to Emma her foundered self-respect.

'Siberia, Emma!'

'The Black Hole, Brownie!'

'The pit behind the pines, Nurse!'

'Eyesore!'

Lorraine asked curiously, 'What evil did you do to get that?'

'I did nothing,' insisted Emma. She was not counting her heady run between the dew-drenched shrubs, for no one had witnessed that. 'I did nothing,' she repeated.

'Then that's why they've sent you down there,' someone suggested smartly.

'Perhaps,' Emma had endeavoured, since no one else was supporting her, 'it's—it's an honour.' Her voice trailed off uncertainly at their pitying glance.

'An honour to leave light and bright for gloom and doom? Why, even Children's after T. and A. would be paradise compared to the Eye Clinic.'

T. and A. was Tonsils and Adenoids, and they all hated it, but at least vomiting and howls were over in a few hours, whereas at EC it would go on much longer than that.

Lorraine, in her uncomfortable way of reading what you were thinking, nodded cruelly at Emma. 'Like the brook,' she smirked, 'for ever.'

'But I can't go on for ever, I mean not at EC. I—I have to graduate.'

'Now you might have hit the nail on the head, Brownie. The powers-that-be don't really believe you'll ever graduate, so heigh-ho, down to the Eye Clinic.'

Emma, in her dejection, almost could have believed this had not the shocked scorn of Sister Stelling remained vividly in her mind. 'A punishment? Our Eye Clinic?' Sister had gasped.

Had she related the incident to the gang, though, they would have pointed out the abnormality of Sister Stelling, for weren't all sisters abnormal? 'You can't make a yardstick of Stelling,' they would have retorted.

So Emma did not speak. But she also refused their kindly if patronizing offers of supper at the canteen and retired early to bed.

'Fit for the fray,' giggled Lorraine.

'Lo,' added Gwyn, 'the conquering hero goes.'

The next morning, not very fit, feeling less a hero than she had ever felt, Emma went correctly along the path instead of over the grass, past the Norfolk pines, down to the atrocity that the hat factory had been too late in snapping up.

No one had told her what time she was expected at EC, but she anticipated it would be the same early hour she always began on Days, taking time off forty minutes after she started for breakfast.

At the bottom of the hill she looked wistfully back at Southern Star. No, this, too, was Southern Star; she must remember that. So, gulping, Emma instead merely looked back.

It seemed like home from here, and she could have opened her arms and run up to it for comfort. Apart from that feeling of belonging, it was, as Lorraine had said that first day, lovely-old, its colonial design achieving with years all the graciousness its ticket-of-leave architect, Francis Greenway, had planned for it, the discreet lines becoming all the more effective under an

Australian sky of indiscreet blue.

Stifling a sigh, Emma turned to her fate.

Trudging through the pine thicket she had planned how she would sweep boldly into EC, storm the citadel as it were, even though anything less a citadel would have been hard to imagine.

But, coming nearer to the Eye Clinic, she saw that this plan could not be carried out. There was only space for slinking, and not even much space for that. The old, dingy, worse-for-wear building evidently bursting its seams had spilled its patients out of the waiting rooms, out of the corridors, out of the lobbies, into the street. There was a queue as far as the bus stop.

Emma hesitated, knowing it was ridiculous for her to join the queue but not seeing how, unless she grew wings and flew, otherwise she could gain entrance.

While she paused someone got behind her, someone else behind them, and she became a queue. Step by step they left the footpath, conquered the lobby, traversed the corridor, and then waited their turn at the inquiry desk.

This was also ridiculous for a nurse assigned to duty, but peering into the cavern-like waiting rooms Emma could glimpse no sisterly figure to refer to, no flying veil to ask, neither there nor in the still dingier wards, or treatment rooms, or whatever the Eye Clinic termed them.

After the light and bright of Southern Star, the gloom and doom of the Clinic made Emma feel abysmal. No wonder then that the harassed desk clerk—who wouldn't be harassed with that queue of people?—looked up, perceived Emma's doldrums, and said briskly, 'An emergency, Nurse? Go right across to Three.' Evidently, despaired Emma, he took her for an eye casualty sent down from Star proper for more detailed treatment.

Feeling quite ridiculous, for joining a queue was an absurd way to begin a nursing day and being mistaken for a case a worse way still, Emma stammered, 'It's not me—I mean it is, but not my eye. I've come to work.' She added in unnecessary explanation, 'I couldn't get through.'

'Back entrance,' he grinned sympathetically. 'Either that or climb through a window, for it's always like this. We could do with ten times the room. No, don't go round now, keep pushing through to Check-Up.'

'Check-Up?'

'After-Op Check-Up for glaucoma, retina detachments, cataracts . . . when you work in such close quarters as this you get to speak the gen. There's sure to be someone there.'

'Where is Check-Up?'

'Down the corridor on the left. The patients'—he grinned again—'will tell you. Sitting on top of each other how couldn't they know?'

Emma stepped back and the woman behind her shuffled forward. I wonder if I'll get into trouble, she wondered, for not having the sense to go by the back door.

Corridors out of corridors seemed to run in every direction, the left to where she had been instructed had its full quota. It was all rather like a spider with a lot of feet and feelers. Where did this feeler lead? To Check-Up?

She asked a patient, and six other patients besides the one she had asked eagerly replied.

'It goes to Pre-Treatment, dear, is that what you wanted?'

'I want Check-Up,' she explained.

'They're so close to each other they're the same. You go along there.'

Emma went along the indicated corridor, becoming more disenchanted with every step. Tiles had left the walls here and there, giving the hall a balding appearance, and glancing up she saw that the ceiling had a quite alarming crack, a window that must have been boarded up years ago was now a mass of buckled plywood, a loud rumble from an ancient air-conditioning plant made a hideous racket.

But at least she saw dark blue and white cuffs, as the sisters at Southern Star wore, and went anxiously forward. As she tried to present herself, for the sister seemed bent on moving in three directions at the one time, Emma could not credit that blue and white could be found here in this dingy spot the same as in the hospital on the hill. She felt almost indignant at the sight.

'Please, Sister—'

'Wait your turn, dear.'

'But, Sister—' Emma's voice was urgent now.

'Down the corridor and along to the right. There's only one, and it's very antiquated, but we're doing nothing to improve it. Once we get to our new EC there'll be a whole block of—Oh, hullo, Nurse, what do you want?'

'Nothing . . . I mean I've been sent here.' Before, like the clerk, the sister could think there was something wrong Emma added, 'Sent to work.'

'Oh, good.' No word about being late, about not having the nous to come the back way, just a thankful gathering up into an evidently insufficient work corps.

Sister said, 'I can manage here, Nurse, if you'll take over Seating.'

'Seating?'

'Retrace your steps to where you came from and the patients will tell you where to go.'

'Yes,' said Emma, only hoping she could retrace her steps as far as the patients.

Again she went distastefully past the balding walls,

under the cracked ceiling, by the buckled window. At least, she admitted, they were landmarks.

'Seating?' she asked of a group already seated and trying to knit in the dingy light.

'Along there and round the corner, dear. Can't miss it.'

'I wish I could,' Emma said as she dodged round more groups who had to stand as there were no more chairs or room for chairs.

More dark blue starch told her she had come the right way. Emma, in her junior butcher stripe uniform and white apron, cuffs, collar and cap, for Southern Star, unlike some of the hospitals now, still stuck to the traditional garb for which the nurses, femininely aware of the subtle flattery of starched skirts, of the twinkling quality of black stockings, were not entirely sorry, stepped forward.

'I've come because—Oh, it's you again, Sister.'

'Yes, I remembered I hadn't told you how, so I took a short cut. After you're here a week you'll learn, too, to be everywhere at once. Now, sort these people out, Nurse, seat them in the order of their pink tickets. They won't like it, they'll want to stop in their groups, and I don't blame them with up to three hours to wait. But with space at a premium as it is here you have to have them in correct rotation. No use calling Mrs Jones and find her in the middle of the row at the back. We've a big attendance this morning, I doubt if you'll find time for tea. By the way, tea's in a corner of the doctors' change room, so cough first. However, you would have known, I expect, and have had tea before you came.'

I didn't even have breakfast, mourned Emma, but she did not tell the sister, who already was moving off.

'I've seated up to number seven,' Sister called back.

'Number eight,' announced Emma in the controlled

but clear voice she had been taught to use at the Southern Star Casualty. But it would not do here, she soon found that out, it simply could not penetrate that babble, that shuffle and most of all that ancient air-conditioning plant.

'*Number eight!*'

'Here, Nurse, but I'll sit with this lady, she's showing me how to do feather and fan, and seeing we have so long to wait—'

'Number eight along the front row, please.'

'But—'

'*Number nine!*'

They grumbled, but they obeyed, for they could see that under these conditions that only strict regulation could prevent chaos.

It was not easy to place them. Several had gone along to the very antiquated room down the corridor where there was only one but where nothing was being done because there was to be a new Eye Clinic, several were clustered round the coffee machine, which, as far as Emma could see, was their sole source of refreshment, and one evidently was deaf and never answered.

She was only up to fifteen when Sister . . . Sister *Morrow*, she learned . . . bustled past to the optical department, or so Emma again learned. Emma, frustrated, feeling that her two and a half years of training, a good part of it most uplifting and impressive, had prepared her for something better than the collecting of tickets, shot her an indignant look.

'I bet it's Alf Croker,' sympathised Sister, pausing a moment and mistaking the indignant look as indignation against an old man taking more than his allotted room while he demonstrated some point to a patient in the row behind. 'He's not deaf, but for all the attention he pays when his number is called you'd think he was. I always alert the one next to him and tell them to give him a prod.'

'How—how long do I do this?' Emma ignored Alfred to ask. She felt her two years plus entitled her to something better than what she was receiving now.

'Until you're through, of course.' Enlightenment briefly touched Sister Morrow, and she smiled crookedly. 'I know how you're feeling, Nurse, but you won't be feeling like that quite soon. Look at me, I always do this job until I get someone to do it for me, and you must admit I'm your senior.'

'Yes, Sister'—docilely—'but couldn't a clerk—'

'My child, one more in this sardine can and the key won't operate. Don't worry, Nurse, the first years are the worst.'

After Alf Croker was coaxed into his right position, his neighbour asked to listen for his name and give him a prod, after the group round the coffee machine were prised away and seated—Emma giving the machine a longing look for all the indifferent brew it appeared to produce—the placing went much easier.

She finished the last row at ten o'clock. Ten was cuppa time up at Southern Star, your seven a.m. breakfast nicely digested and the moment arrived for a second snack—yet I, Emma thought emptily, all this long morning have not eaten one crumb.

She felt horribly hollow, right down to her ankles in the black stockings that she was sure were drooping because of her undernourished legs. She wondered if between the consultant's arrival . . . 'Mr John Harding will be late getting through his quota this morning, he's had a cornea to stitch in' was being babbled along the rows . . . and the ushering in of the patients, she could snatch a cup in the corner of the doctors' change room where you had to cough first.

She edged away, but before she could gain the change room—information as to where it was once more knowledgeably supplied by the patients—a hiss halted her.

'Hi there, Blackie!' the hiss said.

Emma was often called Brownie, being Emma Brown, so turned now and corrected the hiss.

'I meant your *stockings*. Listen, Blackie, give me a lead here.'

It certainly wouldn't have done for Southern Star, where a hovering sister always saw to it that her nurses were correctly approached (even if aprons were untied, other absurdities performed as the miscreants gravely listened), and Emma now stiffened.

The speaker, or rather the hisser, was young and rather dishevelled—dishevelled round the hair, anyway. Strands of untidy locks had fallen over his eyes as though he had been too busy to push them back. For the rest, he was in all white, coat, trousers, shoes. One of *them*, Emma thought. Her gang, awed by the big names that came through the swing doors, names belonging to the lists of consultants inscribed in gold lettering in the vestibule, always spoke of the young, humble Residents as *them*.

'Give me a hand, Blackie,' he repeated.

As Emma still stood, he said, 'I'm to complete these damn forms. I can't ask the sister, she's run off her feet, but I've been watching you, and you've only been stackin' them in.'

Only stackin' them in, indeed! Breaking up the knitting groups, prising away the coffee seekers, bringing back the wanderers from the room up the corridor where there was only one, keeping Croker in place. Only stackin', he said! Emma's cold countenance gave him his answer.

'Thaw out, Blackie,' he appealed, trying to melt her with a warm smile.

It would be falsely warm, Emma knew, knowing young housemen. She found it quite easy to remain cold in a cold passage at half past ten in the morning and still not a crumb inside her.

'Blackie—' he began again, and she icily broke in, 'Brown.'

'How do, Nurse Brown? I'm Harding.'

'Harding?'

'John Harding.'

'John Harding . . . *Mr John Harding?*'

'Doctor,' he said modestly.

'Oh, I know that, but—but *John Harding*!'

Enlightenment flicked over the young doctor's face. 'Not quite. You've got the wrong man, the wrong Dr John.'

'You mean you're not—'

'No, I'm not. I'm new here, this morning—only an hour ago. I've been given these things to do and I haven't a clue. Please help me, Blackie.'

'*Brown*. I, too, am new.'

'But not new today?'

'One hour ago . . . or two, or more.' In her hollowness, Emma was no longer quite sure.

'Oh, horrors! All right, don't stand gawping there and draw attention to my ignorance. Move on, Nurse.'

But Emma did not move. At first her statue-like stance was out of indignation. Never at Southern Star had she been treated like this. And then her immobility was because of something else, of *someone* else—a man, a doctor. A doctor in a coat for all its pristine whiteness less white than the fascinating temple wings of his jet-black hair. A face rather too young for such white wings of hair. The clearest, most searching eyes that Emma had ever seen, blue eyes, deep-seas blue.

She was aware that the untidy-haired person beside her had got to his feet in a hurry and was endeavouring unsuccessfully to swipe back the straying locks.

'Good morning, sir.' The younger man's voice was almost reverent.

'Good morning, doctor. I think it's young Harding, isn't it?'

'Yes, sir.'

'Not only Harding but John Harding—a remarkable coincidence, doctor.'

'Yes, sir.'

'I hope you don't mind?'

'*Mind*, sir?' the wrong Dr John blurted. 'I hope *you* don't mind.'

'On the contrary, I chose you because of it. That's vanity if you like.' A low laugh. 'Well, Dr Harding, settling in?'

'Yes, sir, at least—'

'Yes?'

'Nothing, sir.'

But the way it always is with the great, or so Emma had found, sensing intrinsically now that this man was one of those great, the white-winged doctor had sized up the position and had taken up the troublesome forms.

'Name here . . . eye reading, which you will be doing next, there . . . and so on and so forth.'

'Oh, thank you, Mr Harding.'

So, deduced Emma, here is the great John Harding. She had heard of him, yet never encountered him at Star proper. Waiting silently, she suddenly, enlighteningly knew that EC was the real king, and not the institute of healing up the hill. And it was all because of this man.

'Good morning, Nurse.' His voice cut into her revelation, and Emma felt colour flooding into her cheeks.

How stupid she must look, all pink and flustered, pink went so terribly with bright red hair like hers.

But Mr John Harding stood looking down on her . . . and smiling . . . and recalling. 'It was a good thing I saw her running across the grass,' was what he recalled. 'She is what this place needs. She is what *I* need. Until I have faced up to—what I have to face, she is brightness, colour, light, and until the new clinic rises and the old clinic is tumbled down—'

At that moment, to her horror, Emma was tumbling down. She tried to stop the fall, tried to steady herself with deep breaths, but hollowness had caught up with her, that and a sleepless night last night, and before that a session of troublesome nights including the night of the cot-sawing Beniston.

As from a distance she heard, 'I'll take her.'

Vaguely she was aware she was being carried, and she wondered whether it was the young doctor with untidy hair—or *him*. I hope, she thought, floating in a cotton-wool cloud but beneath the cloud the certainty of strong enclosing arms, it's not Untidy Hair.

But when she opened her eyes in a corner of a small ante-room . . . 'Yes, Nurse, this is our rest nook, also the only space for the fridge for the eye bank, also the one desk used by the doctors for reports and notes' . . . it was to Sister Morrow.

'You,' accused Sister Morrow sternly, 'came without breakfast.'

'Yes, Sister.'

'Here are some sandwiches and a cup of tea. Sorry, but it's all we can ever manage down here. Munch up, then grab more whenever you can between sending the patients in to Mr Harding. Understand?'

'Yes, Sister.'

'And tomorrow morning, Nurse Brown, come *stoked*.'

CHAPTER THREE

It was miraculous what the hot cup of tea and sandwiches did.

In a fairly short time Emma was relieving Sister Morrow again, and controlling the flow in in-patients to the dreary little room where the only thing that was correct was the natural dimness—no need to pull blinds to diminish light in this cavern, but where even the slit-lamp, for want of space, had to be shared with any other visiting medico.

In between seeing his first fifty patients there were notes to be made by the specialist at an inadequate makeshift bench. Later, Emma now knew, the full reports would have to be written at the desk in the ante-room—that is, when the desk was not in use.

It was in use when Emma slipped in for more nourishment . . . she appreciated now the wisdom of building up when opportunity presented itself . . . some time later. Sister Morrow sat there filling in forms.

'This is for our new man, Dr Harding. He's gone on to chart testing now, so I'm lending a hand on these forms. I'm glad you've accepted the advice of frequent replenishing, Nurse. Never, do you hear me, come here unfed again.'

'No, Sister.' Emma took another sandwich. 'How long does Mr Harding keep going?'

'Until he's finished, quite frequently a matter of over two hundred patients.'

'Two hundred?'

'Yes, it's absurd, of course, but all the prelim work

that should be done by someone else can't be for the simple reason that we're already sardines in a tin, as I said before. Even fitting you in, much as you're needed, is a squeeze.'

'But surely Mr Harding can't give his best to all those people?' doubted Emma.

'Mr Harding doesn't deal in anything but the best. I'll not say it wouldn't be better for him with a private room, with questions asked of one pair of ears, but make no error, Nurse, here you only get quality. Oh, well, when we move into our new EC. . .'

'Are we—you getting a new one?'

'Nurse!'

'Oh, I can see a new one is needed, needed urgently, but I just wondered if it was down on the list.'

'Really, Nurse!'

Emma stood censured, considered a moment, and knew she had been remiss. Of course, she recalled too late, all those Saturday fêtes when I served lemonade from the lemonade stall, fished into sawdust for lucky dips, all those flag days, all for PS—'Preserve Sight.' I sold raffle tickets at street corners, but all I thought about was smiling sweetly and trying to beat Lorraine's sales. I never appreciated the reason behind PS. Then she thought: But I do now.

'You better get back to your queue, Nurse.'

As Emma obeyed she glimpsed Dr Harding chart-testing in yet another inadequate corner.

'Hold the card over the left eye,' he was intoning, 'and look in that mirror opposite. What line can you read?'

The man did not respond, and the junior doctor repeated the instructions. Still no reply, and Emma could see that Dr Harding was becoming impatient.

'No, no,' said a quiet voice beside Emma, 'give him time, he's new here.' Mr Harding must have come out to see why the flow into his corner had stopped its rhythm, and Emma went hurriedly back to her brood.

She heard the senior medico explain patiently to the junior that the man, if time did not help him to find the right syllables to read the chart, should be instructed to come next week with an interpreter. The advice was quietly, almost tentatively, offered.

'Never thought of him as being unable to tell me,' John Junior mumbled.

Mr Harding smiled encouragingly, then turned to Emma, inquiring with his deep blue eyes why his flow of patients had stemmed, and Emma said contritely, 'I'm very sorry, sir, the next one is ready to go in now.'

'That's all right, Nurse.' The great man assured it pleasantly.

All right, yet his usher holding up progress with still a hundred patients to go! What a man! What a—

So the morning crept on.

As her benches thinned, as the tension eased, Emma went to stand silently at Mr Harding's door. A little boy was being tested, and as he was pre-school age it was laborious going. He had been given a template and asked to point it up the same direction as the letters in the mirror. Ears up for M, coaxed Mr Harding, feet down for W.

Occasionally the child chuckled, put down the template and made circles instead with his thumbs and first fingers.

'O,' concurred Mr Harding, and chuckled, too.

How can he, marvelled Emma, after one hundred and—

But Dr Harding was not chuckling. He was feeling eyelids now with fingers that were evidently expected to sense primary disturbances. His younger brows than Mr Harding's met together as his fingers traced carefully over closed lids—too carefully in his newness, for he was making no progress.

'Like this.' Again it was Mr Harding, and his long, slim hands were moving across the patient, a little girl not far from frightened tears. At once the child was calm.

Emma's seating was done now, but not her work. And certainly not Mr Harding's.

The great man stood beside her in the ante-room, stood beside the others, and they all drank and ate quickly for the reason there was no inducement here to linger and chatter, and for the stronger reason still that although the queue no longer spilled past the lobby into the street it was none the less a formidable queue.

'Is it always like this?' Emma whispered to Sister.

'Sometimes more, seldom less. Going already sir?' For Mr Harding was turning to the door again. 'No time for a second cup?'

'I'm in Ops now, Sister, I have a little Greek girl I want to examine under anaesthetic.' He flexed and unflexed his long hands.

'The child born without irises?' nodded Sister Morrow.

Here, Emma appreciated, everyone would know what was going on, each case would be everyone's case.

'Yes.' Mr Harding turned in his kindly including way to Emma. 'That is the coloured part of the eye, Nurse.'

'Yes, sir.'

'I want to see if there are any other abnormalities, what chance she has.' He smiled gravely at Emma, and turned away.

When he was gone Sister hustled Emma into an examination room. 'I'm putting you on Drops this afternoon.'

'Can I do it?'

'You'll have to, you can't measure lenses yet, and

that's what I'll be doing failing room to bring someone skilled in.' She sighed. 'You can't go wrong,' she continued. 'You put in these drops after the prelim examination, then wait five minutes and do it again.'

'But there's so many patients and it's dark, I could go wrong and do it three times.'

'You won't, the patient will tell you, and anyway you'll know who's been done by the bright eyes, but don't get carried away by the glitter and do what one of our nurses once did, put some in her own eyes to attract one of the young doctors.'

'Did she?'

'Attract him? She *fell* over him. She was almost blind. That's another point, Nurse, you must counteract the distortion after examination by these normalising drops. And don't let the patient leave until he can see. The locality we're in here, he could go out and be run down by a car. Imagine an EC on a street!'

She bustled off to her lens measuring, and Emma, very uncertain, took up the drops. She was not very good at first, she spilled them down cheeks, on one occasion down the neck of a dress, but she soon got into the way of flicking back the bottle in time and mopping up gently with a tissue.

Looking round her group some hours later, she felt quite safe in stealing away for another snack.

It was while she was pouring a quick cup that she saw the girl in the pink dress going out of the front lobby. She put down the teapot. She's one of mine, she recognised, and she's going off before she should. Even after the normalising drops she should wait for half an hour, and I'm not at all sure I gave her those normalising drops, not with the crowd I've had to deal with and that dim room. I only know by that pink dress that she belonged to me, and now she's gone.

Emma whirled after her. As quickly as she raced, though, the patient was still too speedy for her. How she did it, Emma did not know, for she had seen the effect of the drops on the others, how it had slowed them up even after the prescribed time, how they had had to stop to dab their eyes, blink uncertainly to make sure of their path. But the girl just slipped quickly off the kerb— thank goodness it was a zebra crossing—and almost raced to the other side.

By the time Emma got across, having had to wait to let a stream of cars pass, she could see the pink dress moving quickly towards another street, a street where there was *no* zebra crossing.

Emma fairly raced.

As she ran, she called out, and once she felt sure the pink dress paused, then hastened her pace. What on earth was she playing at, tearing away like that? Evidently, though, it was not a game she was playing, unless it was a game of death, because at the dread street she started across much in the same uncaring manner as before. Several cars screamed to a halt, someone called out. Emma looked round desperately for a policeman, for the way the girl was racing recklessly across she must soon kill herself, but there was no officer in sight. In fact there were few pedestrians at all, this was the motor end of town, not the ways of window-shoppers or city strollers.

'Please stop!' called Emma. 'If you don't stop you'll be run over.' Then: 'You're needed back at the hospital.'

That last, she perceived at once, was a mistake. The pink dress, although now the street climbed quite steeply, fairly raced.

'St—' began Emma, but did not finish it.

'Save your breath, Blackie, I'll run our goose to earth.'

It was the new junior doctor, the wrong Harding, the

one who had called to her—unsuccessfully—to help him
complete the forms, who had waved her impatiently
aside when she had been unable to do so.

Now he was coming to help her, and Emma, too
frantic to be proud, was certainly not going to dismiss
him as he had dismissed her.

'She ran away,' she panted.

'Obviously. What did you do to her? Put the drops
down her throat instead?'

'I did nothing,' gasped Emma at his side, but not at his
side for long, for accelerating his speed he dodged round
the corner of a little tucked-in park and caught the pink
dress just as she was about to tackle another hazardous
crossing.

By the time Emma panted up, the pair were sitting on
a bench and the girl was crying out of her already
reddened eyes.

'I'm going to be blind!'

'You're going to be dead,' corrected the doctor, 'if
you keep on as you've just been going.'

'What's it matter?' the girl mourned.

'Now look here, who told you that you were in such a
bad way? If I remember you took off from the nurse's
department, didn't you? This nurse here.'

The girl did not look, she just mumbled wretchedly,
'Yes.'

'In that case you were only attending an appointment
for refraction. Do you know what refraction is?'

'S-something t-terrible. I only t-thought I n-needed
reading glasses, I never d-dreamed—' More tears.

'Refraction is the separation of an incident ray of light
into two reflected rays,' said Dr Harding, 'the ratio of
the sine of the angle—oh, hell!' He looked at her
helplessly. Then he looked appealing at Emma. 'Tell her
she's a nut,' he said in an aside voice.

'Nice bedside manner,' commended Emma tartly, also in an aside voice. 'The poor child's distraught.'

'So am I after that run. Look, kid'—to the pink girl—'you've got yourself all het up over nothing. Those big words you probably heard, all those instruments, they simply meant—well, they meant—' Again he looked to Emma.

'They meant your eyes are a little shortsighted and must be measured for glasses.' Before any more tears could spurt Emma said quickly, 'What colour frames did you have in mind?'

Nothing she could have said could have mopped up the moisture more rapidly. The flow stopped like magic.

'I thought dark violet and this kind of shape . . . with wide sidepieces so I can flip them off and sort of dangle them. I saw that in a film once.'

Audibly Dr Harding groaned.

Within five minutes they were back at the clinic again, Emma anticipating nothing less than expulsion after her inglorious adventure, and—incredible in one day, one day in the very last spot on earth she ever had wanted to be—she did not want expulsion.

But she was not dismissed, sent back to Southern Star, she was not even censured.

'You poor child,' Sister Morrow sympathised. 'They can lead you a dance, I tell you you have to keep your eyes skinned.'

Mr Harding just gave a kindly smile.

There were no more incidents, and after four o'clock no more patients, but it took up to six to get rid of the ones they had. Even then the clinic did not close.

'Of course not,' said Sister when Emma asked. 'Eye accidents happen at night, too, in fact more frequently at night. Car casualties, night workers in factories—oh, no, we won't shut up at sundown. However, that's not your worry for a while, Nurse, so you can lay down tools and trot up the hill to home.'

Home . . . only this morning she had looked back at Star and thought of it as that. Now, a mere ten hours later, it wasn't any more.

She was glad to go up for a square meal, though, after a day of snacks and cuppas hot food enticed; she thought pleasantly about a long, soaking bath.

'And remember,' called Sister after her as she started off, 'tomorrow come—'

'Stoked,' smiled Emma.

'That'll go for me, too.' Dr Harding had got into step beside Emma. Together they climbed the hill.

There had been animosity between them today, but now, whether it was simply because they were both tired or not, they let the mellow light of the late afternoon slacken their steps and their tempers. They did not speak, they just walked in comfortable silence, nodding briefly at the parting of the ways, Dr Harding to the Residents' quarters, Emma to the Nurses'.

Immediately she was pounced on by the gang. How had it gone? Was it even worse than everyone knew it was? Was she resigning?

Lorraine said acidly, 'With that escort home!' She looked suspiciously at Emma and asked, 'Are views to matrimony rosier down in EC, darling? Was that your reason for asking for a transfer?'

'I never asked,' said Emma, but, escaping the girls, hurrying down for a double helping of everything, running a hot bath much sooner than she should on a full stomach, soaking luxuriously in the bath, she knew that had she been as wise yesterday as she was today she *would* have asked.

'A punishment!' she remembered Sister Stelling. 'At our Eye Clinic!'

No, Emma thought humbly, a *reward*.

CHAPTER FOUR

BUT the next day Emma was not so sure.

From the moment she entered EC—by the back door this time—she knew, from past experience at Southern Star, that it was going to be one of 'those' days. You could never mistake the familiar signs, she thought ruefully, the crowd that for some curious reason were *all* perverse instead of the odd, and expected, perverse one, the things that went wrong, not just things like spilled drops that were going for Sister Morrow, but a procession of things, more important things, though by the look on Sister's face diathol trickling over the old linoleum was no bagatelle.

'Mop it up, Nurse,' she greeted Emma, then added, 'I trust you're stoked this morning, for by the way we've started out we won't be having any time for fainting turns.'

'I had a good breakfast, Sister.'

'And left some on your apron,' Sister snapped, which surprised Emma, for it was not like Sister Morrow, and also the spot, closely checked, was so small only an eagle eye could have identified it.

Sister must have read her thoughts. 'I have an eagle eye,' she sniffed, 'and if I didn't I would wear spectacles, not join the eye exercise class like the thorn at the end of the bench insists on doing. Mr John Harding has explained on numerous occasions that only a certain form of eye refraction lends itself to remedial exercise, that most of us must resign ourselves to glasses, but will she conform? No, she insists on having instruction, and

32

short of disrupting everyone else I have to give in. Anyway'—indignantly—'she has no right to come to EC.'

'Isn't it open for everyone?' Emma, mopping up the drops, asked it in surprise. Southern Star was a public hospital, and seeing this, too, was Star, she had thought the same service would apply.

'It is and it isn't. Though we have no actual rules, because of our obvious overcrowding we expect patients in a more affluent walk of life to go to the doctors in their offices. It makes my blood boil to see that woman taking up the time that should be spent on a deserving case.'

'If she won't agree to glasses surely you would be entitled to show her the door,' said Emma.

'If either of us could see the door. Try and spot it for yourself. If you thought it was busy yesterday, look back on the bare hall that that was compared to today. And all pills, Nurse. Take my word for it, it's going to be like this till six o'clock, and probably long after.' Sister starched off.

A few steps along, however, she starched back.

'When you're finished patient rotation you can take the eye exercise class.'

'What? I mean—well, I mean *what*?'

'What I said. The class that thorn insists on joining. Don't be alarmed, the instructions will be on the desk. It's nothing involved, just a matter of left to right and up and down and winking, even though there's no one to wink back. The children will probably giggle, so you'll have to get their parents to watch, because it will be the parents who will have to keep them exercising each day. It's the third corridor on the right, and take my lady with you, and if she turns cross-eyed it will at least be something achieved.'

'Yes, Sister,' Emma said.

She started unravelling her patients, but, keeping to the early promise of a difficult day, the patients were much more difficult to unravel.

'I can't sit here, it's cold on my kidneys.'

'I can't see to knit here.'

'If we have to wait all that time why can't we wait with our friends?'

'Number Seven,' bellowed Emma mercilessly, and Dr Harding, Wrong Dr John, going along the corridor carrying an eye chart, grinned, 'Blackie, the beast of Eyesore.'

'They have to be in rotation,' Emma defended.

'And don't you love your voice of authority?'

'Oh—oh, shut up!' Emma flung back.

When she turned round again it was to find that Number Nine had changed places with Number Twelve so that she could talk to Thirteen who had changed places with Twenty-four.

'Such regulations,' they grumbled as they were put back.

Emma finished the last seating, took a jealous peep in at Sister Morrow who today was applying the dilatory drops which was performed next door to Mr Harding's room, saw that Mr Harding had not yet arrived, so felt better about collecting her eye exercise class.

'It's along here,' a bored little boy told her. 'Up and down, left and right, round and round, squeeze, blink, a lot of mucky rot.'

'Rot or not, it's going to be done,' said Emma, hurrying along behind the bored little boy. 'Please be seated, class. Parents, kindly observe the exercises, because it will be on your shoulders to supervise them when the children are at home. I trust that anyone who has not been especially directed here realises that only in special cases can eye exercises benefit the sight.' She looked at Sister Morrow's thorn—but found instead a rose. A very beautiful rose. One of the loveliest young women Emma had seen—black-haired, grey-eyed.

The rose looked back without a blink. It appeared patent to Emma that the only blink she would give would be the blink in the eye exercises.

'It is unfortunate but true,' said Emma, reading from a chart on the desk, 'that though the system of exercises known as orthoptic training is of great value in disorders of binocular vision it cannot change the shape of the eyeball, so is ineffective in the correction of long sight, short sight, or astigmatism.' She glanced at the rose, as she was privately calling her, and two beautiful eyes looked calmly back. They certainly, as far as Emma could see, seemed to have the right shape.

'These exercises,' read Emma, glancing up every now and then like a TV news reader, 'aim at teaching the patient to direct his two eyes simultaneously on to a given object and see it stereoscopically.' She had to say that three times, and except that she didn't know a simpler word would have found a substitute.

The small boy grinned delightedly and took the opportunity between Emma's second and third attempt to intone, 'Mucky rot!'

'Exercises,' concluded Emma, 'are valuable in cases of squint and weakness of eye muscles. Now, class, we shall begin.'

'Up and down, left and right, round and round, squeeze, blink,' forestalled the small boy. He had placed himself on the foremost row right in front of Emma. Undoubtedly he was used to all this.

'Kindly go back and sit with your mother,' ordered Emma.

'I can't.'

'Will whoever has this child's place please move up so

he can be supervised by his mother?'

No one moved.

'I can't sit with m'mother,' offered the small boy, 'because she's not here.'

'Then sit with your father.'

'I can't sit with m'father because—'

'Then sit with whoever brought you.'

'I am.' The small boy smiled triumphantly. 'It's me.' At an intentional look in Emma's face he forestalled, 'I brought myself. I come every day because I got to have this mucky rot.'

'Then come and sit with me,' said Emma, and she moved up and squeezed him in. That silenced him, and Emma got on with the job. 'Exercise one: Turn the eyes upward, looking as far as possible without raising the head.' Emma demonstrated, then lowered her gaze to see if the mothers were taking notes.

'Exercise two: Lower the eyes, looking as far down as possible.' She demonstrated again.

'Exercise three: Turn and stretch the eyes far to the left.' This demonstration had the result of Emma looking straight into the gaze of the small boy who was exercising in the opposite direction.

'Mucky ro—' he began, but Emma, looking first furtively around, stopped him with a pinch. He changed 'rot' to 'ouch!'

When the direction was to the right, Emma noted that Mr John Harding had arrived at last. He was in the end room and he was making a note in his memo book. He glanced up, and Emma felt sure he smiled. Then she saw that someone else had seen the specialist and was not bothering to return her gaze to the straight ahead position in order to repeat the exercise. Sister Morrow's thorn was gazing steadily, unswervingly at Mr John Harding.

'Eyes front,' said Emma crossly. It had just occurred to her that that little smile might not have been for Nurse Brown.

'Round and round next,' prompted the small boy, who evidently had forgotten the pinch. He started rolling ecstatically. Emma rolled, too, seeing Mr John Harding at one side of the roll and Dr John Harding at the other side. Wrong John pretended pleased surprise at her noticing him, and rolled back. Fool, thought Emma, he must know I'm only eye-exercising. She looked down at her chart and next superintended squeeze and blink.

Focusing the bridge of the nose which came next was recommended for only two repetitions at a time. 'It should,' read Emma, 'be performed without strain.'

A glance at her class informed her that it was not being performed at all. All eyes were on the small boy beside her who sat transfixed with his own eyes rigidly crossed. He was a terrible sight.

'My mother always did say not to cross your eyes or you'd stop like that,' gasped one of the attending parents.

'The poor child's muscles have gone. What a dreadful thing!'

'Boy,' said Emma, though feeling more like addressing him as horror, 'uncross your eyes at once!'

'I can't, they're stuck.'

The trouble was that Emma did not know whether eyes stuck or not. She knew she could have found out with another pinch, but all the eyes of the class, now that they had uncrossed theirs, were on Emma. It was no use saying, 'Look, this is only my second day, and I don't know whether this child is permanently disfigured or just being a brute.'

'Boy!' she repeated.

'I'm Malcolm.'

'Malcolm—'

At that moment there was a resounding bang, and Malcolm uncrossed his gaze. Everyone relaxed. Emma saw Wrong John Harding outside the door making triumphant gestures and holding aloft a burst paper bag. She should have felt grateful, but he only irritated her. She was more irritated again when she returned her gaze to her class to find that the lovely young woman had gone . . . gone along to Mr John Harding.

A glance at her chart informed Emma that there was a lot more yet . . . eye focusing with a pencil, looking into distance, palming, which consisted of placing the palms over the eyes and relaxing, and which was recommended for at least five minutes. She set them eagerly on this, leapt up and went revengefully after her patient.

But when she got to the door, Emma stopped. The young woman was so near to Mr John Harding she could have been in his arms. Emma tried to reassure herself that most certainly his arms were by his side, but it was poor reassurance.

'Oh, John—John dear—' she heard quite clearly.

'Kristin, I've told you—' Emma must have cast a shadow for at that moment Mr John Harding turned, and there was no doubt that he was pleased to see Emma.

'Nurse?' he smiled.

'My patient,' Emma said back.

The girl mumbled something and went out—but not out to the class.

Emma returned to find her pupils still palming—with the exception of Malcolm, who was emitting piggy snores. This time, as no one was watching, Emma pinched again.

She had thought the pinch unnoticed—except by Malcolm, but snatching coffee around mid-morning, the exercisers, including Malcolm, departed, Wrong John Harding sidled up and insinuated, 'Now I know.'

'That's nice for you,' awarded Emma acidly. 'Knowledge is always a good thing. It should help you to graduate.'

Being one of 'them' he was already well and truly graduated, with the consequence that he went a resentful red. 'Now I know how the kids in Brats get their wounds,' he hissed. 'I used to wonder when I did my rounds and saw all those maltreated little bodies, those purple bruises—*and red pinch marks*—who was responsible.' He paused. 'Now I know.'

'You—' began Emma, more resentful than he had been, for she had been on the receiving end of the bruises and pinches more times than she could remember as she broke up ward fights, 'you—you amateur!'

'Harding MD from the nursing staff.' He put an emphasis on the degree to make sure she appreciated the fact that graduation was now a distant thing.

'A doctor of your *vast* experience,' said Emma, 'must have gathered that the bruises and weals were self-inflicted—at least fellow-inflicted.'

'Today's pinch certainly was not. I witnessed it.'

'Well, what was I to do?' Emma was on the borderline of frustrated tears, and in the blur she did not see that he was grinning.

'A nurse should be quietly cheerful, kind and considerate, never irritable, careless and neglectful. Any more you want to know regarding Patients: Attitude to? Any more questions?'

'Yes. Whose Nursing Manual have you had access to?'

'A little towhead's in first year.' He looked dreamy. 'Pour me more coffee, Blackie. And dry those eyes. Why do you think I burst that bag? I took Orthoptic

Training yesterday and Malcolm on that occasion found he couldn't stop rolling his eyes, but I discovered a way.' He grinned again. 'I pinched him.'

'Poor Malcolm!' Emma was laughing now.

'I wouldn't have minded pinching the brunette,' appreciated Wrong John Harding presently, 'but I'd say, wouldn't you, that she's strictly not for pinching. She and the great Harding—'

'He was taking no notice of her,' put in Emma crossly, and was annoyed by Dr Harding's shrewd whistle.

'That way already, is it? I thought I saw you hot-footing it along the corridor to break up the clinch.'

'There wasn't a clinch, you fool. His arms were right by his side.'

'And do you know why, Blackie? He has a big op this afternoon, and those arms and those hands mustn't be exposed to the least risk. For instance, this would be a risk.' Wrong Dr John demonstrated by encircling Emma with his big arms, a circle from which she indignantly disentangled herself.

'Keep that for your towhead.' Emma added sniffily, 'First year.'

'Snob! All right, Blackie, next time you'll have to ask for it. Seriously, though'—forestalling more indignation from Emma—'Mr Harding wouldn't want pre-pressure of any sort for this job he has coming up. I'—there was an excited note in Wrong John's voice—'will be in on it.'

'How?' Emma asked.

'Well—' John had the grace to look humble—'I'll at least hand something.'

'After Sister Morrow has handed it to you.' For a moment Emma stood daydreaming. Would *she* ever be handing something to Mr John Harding? she wondered.

'Yes,' read Dr Harding shrewdly, 'your heart. And he doesn't need it, dearie, he has more hearts than he can use. He must have—look at the way he let that lovely brunette go. Now your blood pressure's rising again. What a jealous nature! If it's not Harding's brunette, it's my towhead. Look, Blackie, you can't be everybody's girl.'

'When you've finished your cup will you please rinse it.' Emma pushed haughtily out of the room.

Wrong John's teasing laugh followed her out to the corridor, where Sister put her on to preliminary chart reading, which proved not so easy as Emma thought, since there were two pre-alphabet patients, a Greek who could not follow the letters of the Snellen test card and several too-smart teenagers who too-innocently insisted upon pronouncing laboriously the gathered letters of each line.

Next, Emma stood at the door of the dispensary and handed out simple prescriptions. 'We only deal with basic ones,' said Sister Morrow. 'Anything more serious than granulation needs more than what we give out in these little packets.'

'What's in them, Sister?'

'Boracic, mainly, golden eye ointment and agarol—And, Nurse, don't be persuaded in letting any of the teenagers do a double on the agarol. They've found out it's a good eye-shadow, and will come back for more given the chance.'

Mr John Harding had gone upstairs, Dr John Harding had followed. There was a small ward up there, Emma had been told, all ages in together, and only separated for male and female by a curtain. 'Not many eye cases have to stay in hospital,' Sister explained, 'and seeing there'll be ample room in the new EC we're not bothering about enlarging it now. Not that we could.' She stepped nimbly aside to let an orderly go carefully by. 'That's the sort of thing that worries me.' She indicated the orderly moving gingerly down the passage. 'It's too narrow and confined for walking on eggs.'

'What do you mean, Sister?'

'He's taking up the donor eye that Mr Harding is going to stitch in.'

Emma widened her own eyes. She looked spontaneously along the rows.

'Silly child, it was under refrigeration, of course.' Sister Morrow's own eyes fell on a man in the third row awaiting a prescription. 'Did Doctor see you and send you here, Mr Lesmond?'

'No, Sister, but the eye has ulcered again, and last time the black stuff fixed it up.'

'This is one instance when the patient is not after free eye-shadow,' whispered Sister to Emma. She went down to Mr Lesmond and expertly pulled down his eyelid. 'We'll give you more agarol this time, Mr Lesmond, but you'll have to let Doctor see you again. You have a small cyst there, which is causing the ulceration, but it didn't show up before.'

'What'll Doctor do?'

'Just pop it out.'

'I don't think I'd like that,' demurred Mr Lesmond. 'It might encourage it to grow, it could even grow right over my eye. Let sleeping dogs lie, I always say.'

'But your particular dog is irritating you, isn't it? It's not asleep, it's like a little pin that never stops pricking. Don't be a silly man, it's not even as involved as pulling out a tooth.'

'Well—' Mr Lesmond looked less positive of himself and more impressed with Sister.

The corridors were emptying. The intake for each day stopped at ten o'clock, and from then on it took them every available minute to deal with the crowd as well as to be ready for accidents and emergency.

Emma handed out the last prescription, told the last patient to receive normalising drops that she could go now if she promised to go carefully, then went in and brewed Sister Morrow a cup of tea.

'Good gracious, child, I thought you would have been gone. Thanks all the same.' Sister sat down for a moment.

'What about you, Sister? You've been on as long as I have.'

'And will be on longer yet. There's been a baby brought in, and it's been decided to keep him overnight, which means I'll have to stop. We'll be getting you on to that as soon as you've found your feet. It's not all eye nursing in an eye hospital, Nurse.' She yawned. 'I wonder how they're going upstairs.'

'Would they still be going? All this time?'

'Two hours at least to sew in an eye. All that time,' related Sister, 'Mr John Harding won't rest his hands on anything, however tired they are, and the hands have to be rock steady, Nurse.'

Emma thought of Dr John's bantering 'He has a big op this afternoon and those hands mustn't be exposed to the least risk.' He had added, 'For instance, this would be a risk,' and had encircled her. Wrong John Harding was a fool, she thought angrily. Then she remembered how Mr John Harding had not encircled the rose, and felt pleased instead.

But there was nothing foolish about Dr John Harding when he overtook Emma halfway up the hill to home that evening.

'Hi!' he called.

'Hi!' she called back.

He walked in rapt silence, and that so surprised Emma after his bright performances today that she gave him a quick, suspicious look. But he didn't even see it.

'He cut out the diseased cornea and with the finest silk—dyed black so he could see it, Blackie—he stitched the donor cornea in its place with twelve tiny stitches. Then'—John had stopped short under the pine thicket—'a bubble of air was injected between the cornea and the iris to keep them apart. And I,' he finished almost with rapture, 'handed him things.'

This time Emma forbore to interject, 'That Sister Morrow had handed you.' She simply stood with him in the Norfolk pine thicket sharing his thrall.

'Well'—Wrong John emerged from his trance at last—'that's Mr John Harding.' He simply turned on his heel without another word and went.

'Did you and your new boy-friend disagree?' asked Lorraine eagerly when Emma came up the stairs. Evidently she had been watching out and been pleased with what she saw.

'No,' replied Emma in an uplifted voice like Wrong John's had been, knowing she would not be believed but not caring, 'we agreed.'

CHAPTER FIVE

'FROM the sublime to the ridiculous' was what Dr John Harding fumed the following day to Emma when he bumped into her at the end of the third row of the suspected retina detachments. He was, Emma observed, and not without malice, selling tickets for a ham.

'What do they take me for?' he seethed.

'Well, not the ham evidently, seeing that you're trying to dispose of that.'

'Very funny, Blackie.'

'It wasn't meant to be,' proffered Emma humbly, for, as yesterday evening, she found herself in complete agreement again with Wrong John. Probably the agreement was since she was being obliged to be ridiculous after sublime herself. It was scarcely elevating to be taken off dilatory drops followed by normalising drops, presumably entailing a certain degree of responsibility and sense, and being demoted to—Emma consulted her own book of tickets to be sold, then brightened somewhat—a volume of Shakespeare. Well, not such a demotion after all, she smiled.

John saw the upturn of her lips and grew gloomier still.

'What did you get?' he asked.

She showed him.

He refused to be impressed, and said, 'Just the same as I did, only with a "let" at the end of it.'

'There are other plays besides Hamlet,' she reminded him, 'and you must admit the Bard is better than lard.'

'Your funnybone is being over-exercised this morning, Blackie. Can you tell me why we're suffering this indignity?'

'Because,' quoted Emma, 'it is Third Wednesday.'

'Meaning?'

'Today's patient quota,' she told him, having learned all this previously from Sister Morrow, 'has been recommended here from their personal GPs, they haven't just come along because their pockets aren't jingling and they can't afford a specialist.'

'Meaning again?'

Emma said in a very low voice so that her ticket victims would not hear, 'Probably they have more money than our customers on the other days.'

'Meaning finally?'

'That every Third Wednesday we sell tickets.'

'Who—you and I?'

'Anyone who can be spared.'

'For what cause?'

At this Emma borrowed Sister Morrow's shocked tone on her first day at the clinic when she vaguely had asked Sister: 'Are you getting a new EC?' But instead of a hurt 'Nurse!' she said a horrified 'Doctor!'

He looked back at her, then clicked his tongue. 'The fêtes and bazaars and flag days—of course! I thought they were only put on to give you nurses something to do.'

It was Emma's turn to be horrified, and she was.

'Something to do, indeed! Let me tell you now that—'

'Is there a second prize, dear?' asked an old lady waiting her turn to go in for examination.

John seized Emma's book and turned the pages triumphantly. 'By the look of your sales there won't be any prize. The whole thing will be called off, you've barely sold any. I must have a better bedside manner, I've nearly got through my quota.'

'No credit to you but to the pig.' Emma looked disgustedly at her own book. 'Food for food always appeals more than food for thought.'

'So says Envious Emma. That is your name, I hear.'

'Yes, Jubilant John,' answered Emma sarcastically. 'Nineteen tickets sold for a ham to my humble three for Hamlet.' She gave a mock gesture of humility and started on the next row.

For all his superiority in salesmanship, though, Dr Harding did not look any happier when she met him at the end of the fourth row. Emma knew why. She knew he was resenting each of the visiting medicos now cloistered in the retina department with Mr Harding, she knew he was aching to be in there as well.

'I suppose all this is for a good purpose,' he gloomed. 'I suppose one day when I'm stitching in an eye in a special sterile streamlined treatment room in the new EC I'll be glad I sold tickets for a ham to make it all possible.'

'Will you be there?' she asked.

'What makes you doubt it, Nurse?' he retorted.

'I wasn't doubting,' she calmed him down, 'I was just wondering whether you intended sticking to eyes or going on to something else.'

'Last night there was no doubt in me. Now—' John started on the next row.

She did not see him at the end of the fifth. Halfway along Sister Morrow beckoned him to go in by Mr Harding's special invitation to watch the procedure. 'But no hurry,' added Sister, 'finish your tickets first.'

Dr John pulled a note from his pocket and piled it and his book on to Emma. 'Write off the lot,' he said rapturously, and hurried off. A little disgruntled, for it appeared there was to be no escape for her, Emma wrote up his money on the butts. She finished her own book at last and Sister Morrow found some filing for her to do.

'I sell tickets often myself, Nurse,' Sister stated astringently, 'so there's no need to wear that long face.'

'Dr Harding didn't have to finish his, though, I see.'

'Naturally. He will possibly be doing one day what he has gone in to watch, so it's never too early to experience the facts.'

Emma thought that over as she filed. Filing finished, she dusted, and absently took up the dilatory drops. She wondered what they felt like, and thought that this was as good a time as any to find out. After all, if you treat a patient with them you should know what he is experiencing. She knew Sister would disapprove, having mentioned this sort of thing before, but if Dr John Harding was allowed to experience the facts, Nurse Brown should, too.

She put them in.

Nothing particular happened, except that she would not have liked to have been asked to read the test card. She peered at her eyes in the mirror and saw that they were starry. She wished Mr Harding would come out for a moment, but that, by the dedicated silence in the treatment room, was unlikely. She did some more dusting, then put in the normaliser.

Her eyes were still glistening, though, when Dr Harding emerged, glistening himself.

'The doubt has gone, Nurse Black,' he burst forth at once.

'Nurse Brown,' she corrected.

'I referred to your legs.'

'They don't nurse,' she said pettishly.

'Well, they carry you, don't they, and you are a nurse, aren't you? Or'—Wrong John gave her a dubious look— 'are you? A nurse is—'

'Quietly cheerful, kind, considerate, never irritable, careless and neglectful,' quoted Emma. 'In what category have I failed?'

'You were inconsiderate, you deliberately interrupted me with a frivolity, you said Black instead of Brown.'

'It was Brown instead of Black, and I don't consider my name a frivolity.'

'Well,' said Wrong John carelessly, 'it's unimportant, anyway, you'll only change it. You'll be Mrs Jones or Smith or—'

'Mrs John Harding.' It came out by itself, she was not aware of saying it. Luckily, she thought guiltily, she had barely mouthed it, but, seeing the expression on Dr Harding's face, of course, Big Ears had to hear.

'Don't be a nit,' he withered.

'All right then, Mrs Dr John Harding,' Emma snapped, annoyed with herself, more annoyed with him.

'I'd have to get used to that idea,' Wrong John said in a tasting sort of voice.

'Oh, you fool!'

'No, you're the fool,' he interrupted, 'stepping on my dreams. Never do that again, Blackie. I rushed out to tell you all about the detached retina and you interrupt me over a colour.'

'Well, it's been all right for you,' Emma grouched, 'you've been learning.' Almost she had said, 'You've been with *him*.' Plaintively she mourned, 'I've just been selling tickets, and filing, and—' She stopped cautiously, darting a quick glance in the direction of the drops. Had she replaced them safely? She had—but her glance was not quick enough in returning.

'Uh-huh,' pounced John, 'you've been sampling the wares. I bet when you were up the hill you used to dab your face with ether. Good for the skin, my towhead tells me, discourages pimples.'

'I did nothing of the sort. Unlike your junior nurse I had no pimples.'

'Only dimples,' he said fatuously. 'Little Emma Dimples. Look, Nurse Dimples, if you ever touch those drops again—' He stopped. 'You do look a bit starry, though. So much so that I'm going to extend an invitation.'

'To what?'

'Tonight's hop. In the Welfare Hall.'

'I decline.'

'You can't, you know, it's for EC, and it's obligatory to attend.'

'Obligatory for—for principals, too?'

'Be assured, my child, that Mr Harding will also be there. But be assured at the same time that he will not be inviting you.'

Emma stood silent.

'I'm serious, Blackie,' said Wrong John. 'I have to go, and EC, so Sister informs me, prefer their staff to go with each other. A sort of ad for the place. I have no one else to ask.'

'Thank you.'

'Also,' went on John, 'you have no one else to ask you.'

'Thank you again.'

'Then you'll come?'

'It seems,' said Emma bitterly, 'I have no choice.'

'I'll put it down in my little black book,' he promised, then wiped the banter—and Emma—aside as the visiting doctors began coming out of the retina room. At the end came Mr Harding.

Sister Morrow bustled up with the news that a pebble from a lawn-mower case had been brought in.

'Is it already spring?' asked Mr Harding in surprise. He turned and included Emma as always in the conversation. 'Spring, Nurse,' he smiled, 'always brings in our pebbles from the lawn-mowers. Through the winter the grass does not grow, but as soon as the greening comes in come the injured eyes.'

'This is only a minor blow,' reported Sister, 'luckily there's no puncture.'

'Then I think we'll send you, Doctor,' Mr Harding smiled at Wrong John.

'Yes, sir,' agreed the junior man eagerly, and was down the corridor in front of Sister before she could lead the way.

'The enthusiasm of youth,' Mr Harding smiled again. 'Tell me, Nurse, are you enthusiastic?'

'I—I don't know—I mean, sir, in what capacity?'

'May I show you?'

'Oh, yes, please.'

'Then come along.' He walked towards the front door.

'Can I—I mean I'm still on duty—I mean, sir, where are you taking me?'

'Somewhere that could be considered in the line of duty, Nurse: along to the new EC.'

'Oh!'

'You've seen it?'

'No—I mean—' Even if she had seen it, and not having paid much attention before she was uncertain, it had not been with *him*. 'I mean no, sir,' she hastened to reassure.

'Then come along.' He held the door open for Emma to pass through, and as he did so his long thin fingers touched her arm and she was aware of a quickening pulse. Side by side they walked down a little, up a little, and then stopped.

Now that she stood beside Mr John Harding and looked at the new edifice it seemed impossible to Emma that she had not watched—and loved—every rising brick of it as she was aware by his proud stance that the man with her had watched and loved.

But in the days before she had known Mr Harding it had simply been some hospital project or other that was going on, something moreover beyond the Norfolk pines which made it beyond the pale, of course.

How wrong she had been! And how fully she realised it now! She saw the ambitious height of it, the capacious width of it, with a deep new elation. 'Gather hope,' she said impulsively aloud, 'all ye who enter here.'

The man beside her turned quickly and smiled. 'You read my thoughts, Nurse. Thank you for giving them voice. Gather hope.' He looked up at the building.

They stood silent a long moment, but in the silence Emma felt very near to him; she felt akin. It was a feeling she had never known before, and she felt a rush of warm tears. She looked up at him through the blur, then blinked the tears away. *For Mr Harding's eyes were tear-glittering, too.* She felt sure of it.

'Sir—'

He gave an odd little gesture of denial, brushed his hand across his eyes. And the tear-glitter with it?

'A fine building, Nurse,' he said a little huskily.

'Very fine, sir. Sir—' She wanted to say, Why are you sad, then, for all your pride, for I feel you are, I'm sure you are, can I know?

'Nurse?'

'Sir—it will be good for you here, won't it?' she murmured for something to say, something to hide the question trembling on her lips. She was totally unprepared for the crumpling in him—yes, she could only call it crumpling. He turned away and did not speak for several minutes.

Then—'It will be very good for those privileged to

work here, Nurse.' He began pointing out the different sections, he did it briskly. 'Reception, would you say, Nurse? Emergency in that wing? Casualty over there?' He went on quickly, enthusiastically. But something was wrong, and Emma sensed it. His heart, for all that previous pride of stance, that infectious zeal, was not now in his voice or gesture. Something was *very* wrong.

Abruptly in the middle of his demonstrating he stopped and said, 'Shall we go back?'

Emma got in step beside him, and they went back towards the old EC.

His abstraction at last must have become noticeable even to him, for he said suddenly, 'I'm sorry, Nurse.'

'It's all right—I mean—' Not knowing what to say, she let her words trail off.

'Look.' He stopped short and stopped Emma with him. 'The dance for the new clinic tonight, generally I just look in at functions, I'm not a social man, but would you do me the honour of coming with me, Nurse?'

'I—with you? I mean—'

'Is it that terrible?' He was laughing now. 'Am I that old?'

'Oh, no, no, you're not old, but you're—very important.' As she said it Emma wished—too late—that it was the only thing that could stop her. But as well as his importance, which undoubtedly he would waive aside, there was a previous agreement with Junior back at the Eyesore. Oh, bother Dr Harding!

'You flatter me.' He smiled and bowed to her. 'But you will come?'

'No. I mean I am going, but—'

'Of course, child. Ridiculous of me to have asked. My young namesake, of course.'

'Yes,' Emma said unwillingly. All heaven in her reach, but she was deprived because someone else had asked first, asked because there was no one else to ask, had advised her to accept because there was no one else to ask her. Or so he, Dr John, Wrong John, had said. Oh, the irony of it! To think that if she had not agreed to small-time she could have, could have—

'Perhaps, Nurse,' said Mr Harding, 'I can have one dance.'

'Oh, yes, yes.' All of them if you like, she wanted to add. He, that *boy*, is only taking me because there's no one else.

He was smiling down on her, and Emma smiled a little wanly back. He's wonderful, she was thinking, he's everything, *and I could have gone with him*.

But Mr John Harding was only thinking: she is all brightness, all colour, all hope. All the swift things.

'Thank you for looking at the new clinic with me, Nurse.'

'Thank you for taking me, sir.'

'*Gather*, not abandon hope, you said?' He nodded along to the rising building.

Emma nodded back.

'Thank you,' he said again, and turned left once inside the old EC portals to the office-tea-change room to write up his notes.

Emma went along to see if she was required for anything else. Tonight, she was thinking rapturously, tonight, tonight, even though it's only one dance. What will I wear? Will I have time to do my hair?

'Those drops should have worked out of your eyes by this time.' Dr Harding met her in the corridor and gave her a searching look. 'Or are they still starry because you're coming out with me?'

'Quite the opposite.'

He took out his little black book. 'But you are; I recorded it.'

'I meant you have quite the opposite effect on me.'

'No stars, you mean, Blackie. Well, so long as I have some effect—I'd hate to be ineffective. If you're ready to knock off, Nurse Dimples. I'll walk you up the hill.' But it was down a little, up a little once again with Mr Harding that Emma's heart yearned for. Still, she thought, that dance tonight. Visibly she glowed.

'There *are* stars. How many drops did you put in? Do you think you can walk a straight line?' It was Wrong John again.

'Without your help,' snapped Emma crossly, coming to earth again, brushing off his extended arm.

Not that he could have helped her even had she permitted it. At the doorway Sister Morrow called busily, 'Oh, Dr Harding! Congratulations, you won the ham.'

'I—but—oh, heavens!' For the ham was large and pink and not unlike a big bare leg, and where was a houseman to put it?

'I donate it back,' said Dr Harding grandly.

'Another three weeks in this sardine can? Don't be ridiculous. I'm going up to my baby now—yes, it's still in—and don't let that ham be here when I come down.' Sister Morrow marched off, leaving Wrong John holding the body.

'Blackie, rustle up some wrapping,' he begged.

'Rustle up your own,' giggled Emma, making happily for the door. Really, this made her day complete! 'It's your fault,' she called, 'buying all those tickets.'

'It's your fault putting my name down. Why couldn't you just have left the butts blank, you nit?'

'Goodbye,' trilled Emma, '*both* of you.'

She brushed past Wrong John and the big pink form and ran up the hill to get ready for *one* dance.

CHAPTER SIX

THE pink cotton or the blue pleats, the twirly chiffon or the silk dress? And what to do to her hair?

Emma stood in front of a clouded bathroom mirror, clouded by the scented mists arising from the steaming waters, the scent arising in its turn from half a bottle of jasmine crystals left behind by Maree who had been the last bather. When Maree returned for her bottle she was not going to be pleased.

But Emma did not care. She did not care if everyone in the world was displeased—except *him*. Pink, blue, twirls, slenderness? What was the pleasure of Mr John Harding—the Right John?

She piled her red hair on top of her head, she tried it swinging loose, she swept it aside in a French roll, she made a pageboy of it.

'Emma, for heaven's sake, are you drowned?'

'Hurry up in there, I want to come in!'

Emma jumped in the scented bath, leapt out again—a shocking waste of Maree's crystals, she thought—talced, put on her dressing-gown and made way for an indignant Clarissa.

'Selfish pig,' said Clarissa in passing, 'why can't you have your face-pack outside like the rest?'

'I didn't do a face-pack.'

'Well, not that you'd notice either way.' Clarissa locked the bathroom door.

Maree knocked on it in vain for her bath crystals, and Emma consoled herself that at least she wouldn't get her rightful blame for that. Clarissa would.

And Emma saw at once that she needed consolation. The only barely adequate mirror, since Southern Star, having been erected in the days when women did not look, or were supposed not to look, at their reflections, was deficient in mirrors, was completely blotted out by thirty preening creatures. At least they would have preened had they had room. Every inch of the glass was filled with round faces, square faces, black hair, blonde hair, quite a few sandy heads, though not one flame-red like Emma's. Girls shoving, pushing, combing, powdering, borrowing, exchanging, giggling, confiding, accusing, sulking.

But no space left.

Disconsolately Emma took to the small slit mirror above the hat stand, climbing at once on a chair to see if that vague spot on her chin was about to change Nurse Dimples to Pimples—a horrible thought, and one that might never have occurred to her had Wrong John not brought the matter up.

'Anyone,' she called as she peered, 'know a first-year towhead in tow with houseman Harding?'

'*Your* Harding?' asked Lorraine.

'Oh, no, not—' She had been about to say, 'Not that Harding,' but stopped herself. If she had uttered it, she thought, the mirth would be on. A simple mid-way, a flaming redhead at that, setting her junior cap at no less a personage than the great Mr Harding! If they only knew, thought Emma, climbing down again . . . it wasn't what Wrong John had said but an undissolved crystal attached to her skin . . . if they only knew he had actually asked her tonight.

'I've seen her,' proffered Lorraine, 'pale, fair and cool.' She looked pointedly at Emma's far from cool head.

Maree was waiting her chance to get into the bathroom where Clarissa was now splashing. 'I left my expensive crystals in there,' she wailed.

Emma hurriedly removed her mauve 'pimple.'

'Is the hall decorated?' she asked anxiously. It must be nice, she was fretting, it must be very nice—for *him*.

'As usual,' said Helen indistinctly because she was tracing round a lipstick pencil.

'Plastic roses,' objected Emma.

'What else? It's only a hop like we have every month.'

Only a hop . . . That was what she had thought too, once . . . but that was in the olden times, exactly two days ago. pre-EC. Only a hop, indeed!

'It's for such a good cause,' she heard herself babbling. 'Every brick that rises means more than a brick, it means Gather hope all ye who enter here.'

For a moment the thirty paused, turned and looked at her.

'Are you going all dedicated, Emma?'

'Has the Black Hole performed black magic?'

Lorraine said shrewdly, 'Are you in love?'

'Of course not!' sharply.

'Methinks the lady doth protest too much. Congratulations, Brownie, the first of us to snare an MD.'

'I haven't. I mean—'

'You mean it's not signed, sealed and delivered yet?'

'She could mean she's out for more letters than MD. What about John Harding's namesake, the great Mr John?' They all laughed at the very idea of that, and the matter, thank heaven, passed over. But, thought Emma, if they only knew who had asked whom.

In a bunch, satisfied at last with what the mirror reported, the girls, moved out, thirty butcher-boy-striped nurses emerged from their starchy chrysalises to soft butterflies of every colour, blue, green, golden . . .

and that brought back Emma's problem. What was she to wear?

There was no hurry. Seeing Wrong John had invited her he would pick her up, and it would do him good to cool his heels in the corridor. Emma tried three dresses, four hair-do's, by which time Wrong John still had not arrived but the orchestra had. She could hear the music floating up from downstairs, and one of the dances they were playing could be hers with the Right John.

She stood tapping her feet anxiously, looking at her watch angrily. If Wrong John didn't come soon it would be supper, and after that there were few dances left, for the hospital hops stopped strictly at eleven-thirty in order that there would be no Tired Tims on Mornings. How dared the man invite her and then not turn up! 'I'll put diathol in his tea,' she seethed, noting with interest that she had already got into the way of talking in eye gen instead of lungs and stomachs. 'I'll—I'll—'

There was a tap.

Emma fairly flew to the door. 'And about time, too!' she greeted hotly. 'Who do you think you are . . . oh—oh, Mr Harding!'

'So you're ready.' The Right John bowed formally and smiled. 'When you weren't in the hall I wondered if something had gone wrong.'

'*You* wondered?'

'Why not? After all, you had promised me a dance.' He bowed again, and extended his arm. How wonderful his silver-edged hair looked with his formal black and white dinner suit, and how wonderful a dinner suit would look in a hall of casual jeans, for that was all the men ever wore to the monthly hops, though of course Mr Harding would be expected to be different, being the founder of it all. Almost in a trance, Emma slipped her arm in his.

'You look very charming, Nurse.'

Did she? She couldn't remember what she finally had settled on, and was her hair up or down?

'I'm glad you like pink with red,' she murmured.

'Pink with red?'

'Lots of people don't, it clashes, they say.'

'Clashes?'

'My hair,' she reminded him. 'It's red.'

'Titian,' he corrected. Then he asked in puzzlement, 'Pink?'

'My—' She looked down and saw that she had changed from the pink after all into green. Inadequately she mumbled, 'All flushed after the hurry of getting dressed—I mean it makes you pink and red.' She thought how silly she must sound.

'A hurry?' He asked it gently. 'The other nurses have been down half an hour.'

'And so would I if Wrong John had turned up as an escort should.'

'Wrong John, Nurse?'

Oh, her tongue again! Emma inwardly berated herself and said weakly, 'Young Dr Harding.'

'Ah, my namesake. But why "wrong"?'

'Just—just a tag he has,' she said too casually.

'A common tag—or yours?'

'Mine.' There was something about Mr Harding that made you answer the truth.

'And why is he wrong?'

Before she could think Emma answered, 'Because he's not you.'

There was a little pause. Then Mr Harding said, quite oddly, Emma thought, 'That, in my book, would make him right.'

'No—*you* are right.' Once more she spoke without thinking first.

The silver-winged man looked down at her with those deep seas blue eyes and there was a little sadness there. 'If only that *was* right, Nurse. But thank you, anyway. Here we are now. Before your escort claims you may I claim my dance?'

It was a grand entry and well worth every minute of her impatient foot-tapping upstairs. Every head turned to look at them . . . Emma hoped *his* wretched head had turned, too, Wrong John's head.

Mr Harding danced smoothly, he danced well enough to talk and not concentrate on his steps. ·

'How have you settled in, Nurse?'

'The Eyesore . . . oh, I'm sorry, EC?'

A little smile. 'Yes.'

'I—I think I've been waiting all my life for it,' Emma said.

Another turn round the floor, then Mr Harding asking, 'What do you intend doing with that life, Nurse?'

She glanced up at him, then down again. She had never really thought much about the future, except in terms of a pleasant house somewhere, a nice-looking if at present nebulous husband, a bunch of cute children, not a concentration of thought as Lorraine practised, just an inevitable idea that that was how it would be in the end, but now—now she felt differently. She felt dedicated, as dedicated Megan was . . . Megan was the one in their batch who was going on for higher things.

'I want to give my all to nursing.' Megan said that often, so it came parrot-wise to Emma's lips. All the same she felt she meant it, in the great John Harding's arms she *knew* she meant it.

'Not all, Nurse,' he was advising, 'never give all.' His voice was not just kind, it was concerned.

'Sir?'

'Because then if anything—happened to your career, then nothing would be left.'

'But I don't understand.'

'Then that's good,' he nodded. 'It's—kinder. Just remember, Nurse, never give all.'

'But you give all.'

'It *was* my idea.' He cut short a sigh, but not before Emma heard.

The rest of the dance was danced in silence. For all her rapture that she was dancing with the great Mr Harding, the Right John, Emma felt inexplicably sad. It was the same sadness that she had sensed this afternoon when she had stood with the specialist looking on the rising edifice of the new Eye Clinic, sensing something in the great man that grieved her because it grieved him.

She wetted her lips. She would say something, something that would break through to him like—like birds singing, like sunshine after rain, like—

'John!' The clear voice penetrated the last note of the waltz, the last shuffle of feet in a final step, and the thorn, really the rose, Wrong John's glorious brunette, came across and took her partner's arm.

'Kristin! You here!'

'Why not? It's all for the cause, isn't it, and it doesn't have to be confined to staff?'

'No, but—'

A sweet pout . . . she really was very pretty . . . and then a kindly, 'Someone's beckoning you, Nurse' to Emma.

Emma glanced across and saw it was Wrong John, so she turned the other way. She not only turned, she left. She had just had a beautiful idea.

Sister Morrow was not there, she was looking after the baby who had been detained for another night, and suddenly, in spite of Mr Harding's advice, service, devotion, was what Emma wanted, too. I'll never marry, she decided, the nebulous husband receding, the cute children dissolving, the charming house taking on the walls of a hospital, remarkably like what the finished walls of the new EC should be. Somewhere in the vestibule stood a figure remarkably like Mr Harding. Dedication! It swelled in Emma. She increased her pace towards the Black Hole, much blacker again by night.

'Hi, Blackie!' halted a voice.

Before Emma could collect herself and start off again, the owner of the voice had caught her up. 'Where do you think you're going, Nurse Dimples, because you're jolly well not. This is my dance—that is if you can bring yourself to go slumming after the mighty John Harding.'

'But for Mr Harding I wouldn't be here,' stormed Emma, remembering how she had stood tapping her feet and consulting her watch, and waiting for a laggard escort.

'Don't tell me,' said Wrong John, 'he was your mother's obstetrician.'

'He called for me—a thing, incidentally, which you either forgot or refrained to do.'

'Refrained is the word, Blackie. To put it brutally, when I asked you this afternoon I only thought it was nominal.'

'Nominal?'

'That I met you in the hall.'

'You really mean you didn't intend to pay for me?'

'That's it,' he grinned.

'But—but good gracious, haven't you ever taken a girl out before?'

'Plenty. Remember that first-year towhead I told you of.'

'And haven't you paid for them?'

'But didn't,' he reminded her sourly, 'I have the money to pay?'

'You mean you haven't now?'

'I mean I have instead one pink ham. All my ready cash has gone on that. At least I did have one pink ham.'

'What do you mean, you did?'

'I donated it,' said Wrong John, 'back to the fund, and they're drawing it after the last dance.'

'But you can't have spent all your money on those tickets.'

'Can't I? I have.' Before she could interrupt he said reproachfully, 'It was all I had till pay day, and you squandered that note on butts on which every name you inscribed was mine.'

'Shows you I think about you.'

'What thoughts!' he flung back. 'All right, are you ready for our dance?'

'No. I'm going to work.'

'What?'

'I'm going to EC to relieve Sister Morrow. She's had a baby.'

'By jove, that's sudden. I wouldn't have thought so this afternoon.'

'She has a baby to look after tonight and I'm going to watch it while she comes up here for a few minutes. I know she'd like that.'

'And you'd like it, too,' he said shrewdly. 'Is it maternal instinct, Blackie, or did your last dancing partner light a candle in your heart?'

'My last dancing partner was my only dancing partner, thanks to you.'

'Well, we'll fix that right now.' He took her arm and started to whirl her around.

'Stop it, you fool,' she said angrily, pulling away from him.

'Only the leaves will see,' he promised, for the short whirl had brought them beneath the enveloping Norfolk pines. 'In which case—' he added. He pulled her to him and implanted a kiss.

Ordinarily Emma would not have taken much notice. Kisses were kisses, in fact for status' sake rather to be desired, especially from a houseman. But *now*, just after Mr John Harding, the Right John—

'Go away,' fumed Emma, and shoved, shoved hard.

She followed up the shove by running in the direction of EC, and, temporarily put off his balance, Wrong John did not catch her, particularly when he had to wait at the zebra crossing and she got across straight away.

By the time he went through the door, the vestibule looking oddly bare by night without its queues of patients, Emma was climbing the stairs to the ward.

She hadn't been in the ward before, and its meagreness rather shocked her. Just essentials, nothing else, but what would be the use when the idea was not to expand but to disband. Sister Morrow was seated at a desk, and rather breathlessly Emma hurried across to her.

'Sister, I want you to go up . . . I mean I can watch here . . . I mean you're so interested . . . I mean all the staff has been represented except you.'

Sister looked surprised, eager and censorious at the same time, surprised at Emma's entry, eager to go, censorious that a junior could actually think she could take over from a senior.

'Yes, we thought we'd give you a break.' Dr Harding was now by Emma's side, so of course it would be all right, thought Sister Morrow.

'It's very nice of you both,' she praised, looking pleased now.

But Emma was not pleased, all her dedication had

gone. She glowered at Wrong John, taking care that Sister did not see, for obviously she was anxious to have a look in at the dance in aid of the cause.

'We've only three overnight,' she instructed briskly, 'the donor eye behind the screen—the screen's because he's male, though the poor fellow's bound up, of course—Mrs Wright who had a tear duct op this morning, and Gregory.'

'The baby?'

'Yes.'

'What's wrong with Gregory?'

'Cataracts.' Sister Morrow got up, straightened her veil, put on her red cape and started off. 'I won't be long,' she promised.

Wrong John urged, 'Take as long as you like.' He glanced promptingly at Emma. 'That right, Blackie?'

'Take as long as you like,' echoed Emma with less enthusiasm, but she hoped it didn't show.

'I'll do nothing of the sort,' promised Sister Morrow. 'Even though I'm past last dances I can still remember how important they were.'

On which smiling note she left.

'Last dances.' Wrong John spoke first. 'We had no dance at all, unless you count that polka under the pines, though to me it seemed more of a shove.'

'It was a shove.'

'Why, Black? Why did you shove me?'

'You know very well,' she snapped, 'and keep your voice down.'

She tiptoed across to the bandaged baby, who appeared to be sleeping peacefully. 'Surely not cataracts?' she murmured more to herself.

'I can help you there.' Wrong John's voice did not banter now. 'It's cataracts, Nurse.'

'But his age—'

'Has nothing to do with it. As it happens, Emma, I'm in this game now because of—well, because of a thing like this.' He nodded to the white bandage. 'He was my sister's boy.'

'He *was*, you said. Does that mean—you mean he—'

'No, I don't mean it like that, I mean he was in a state like this child is, but now he's all right.'

'Gregory will be all right?' she asked eagerly.

'I think he should—after Jason. Jason is my nephew. He was always a fine youngster, except—' Wrong John hunched his shoulders. 'Ever seen cataracts in a kid, Emma? Little, no, almost miniature white pebbles, behind which the young 'un peers and peeps. It bruises you.' He said it briefly. 'It bruised me. It bruised me so much I left engineering . . . you know what, I always wanted to build bridges . . . and took on sawbones instead. But only with this in view, with eyes in view, Emma, because I had seen the miracle of Jason coming out from behind his little white pebbles and looking fully at things at last.'

Emma nodded, waiting for him to go on.

'It took time, because it had to be one cataract at a time, one eye at a time.' He laughed softly. 'It's a funny thing, Emma, but it's the inconsequential things in medicine that move you most. Young Jason saying one day in a usually busy street that was undergoing a temporary slack and lull: "All the people must be lying down for their drops." That's the world he lived in, three times a day down on the cot for drops.'

'But he's better now?'

'He's fine. He has to wear glasses, of course. I'll never forget the day Joan . . . my sister . . . brought him home from a local baby show with the elation prize.'

'Elation?' she queried.

'Consolation, really. Every kid who didn't get the

Championship Cup got one. But Joan's was elation, not consolation, because for the first time in years she had not hurried him away from other people, stood between him and kindly but maddening sympathisers, she actually had put Jason in the baby comp, specs and all.'

'And he took,' breathed Emma, 'the Elation Prize.'

A little silence fell between them. It was the nearest . . . apart from that initial evening of their meeting when, tired but replete, they had ascended the hill together after their day's work was done . . . that they had been since they had met.

When the little boy whimpered in his sleep and Emma took him from the cot and nursed him, they seemed to become an entirety, not three parts.

They were still sitting like that when Sister Morrow came back, and she thought they made such a nice tableau that she refrained from telling Emma that a nurse should not take a child up just because he whimpered, that a general soothing would do, that it would only make a rod for some other nurse's back. She refrained from telling Dr Harding that he should have known—and instructed—that.

'Time, if you run, for the last dance,' she smiled.

They didn't run. They walked up the hill together, side by side, hands brushing when the path narrowed under the pines.

It was under the pines he had kissed her and she had shoved him away, thought Emma, thinking more kindly of Wrong John now, not kissing-kindly but on the other hand not planning any more shoves.

He gave her no cause, though, still with their hands touching whenever they brushed together, still tied invisibly by the thought of small Gregory in his bandages, Greg who one day, like Jason, might win his mother an Elation Prize, they went companionably into the hall.

The companionship lasted exactly one minute. The drawing of the ham was taking place. 'Donated by Houseman Harding,' intoned the voice through the microphone, 'who also . . . thank you, Doctor . . . bought the bulk, if not all, of the tickets. We've had a lot of raffles tonight, so I don't suppose I can reproach the rest of you for patronising the whisky before the ham, though a lovely ham it is'—he held aloft the bare pink leg—'and I'm sure'—he looked at the piece of paper that had been handed to him—'Nurse Black will enjoy every mouthful. Where are you, Nurse Black?'

Emma stood still, and would have remained still had she not been impelled forward by Wrong John. 'Here she is!' he called.

'I'm Brown, not Black,' protested Emma, but everyone giggled, especially the girls.

'You look a pretty pink to me,' awarded the man behind the microphone, 'even a prettier pink than the ham you've won. Now you've spoiled it, you've gone red.'

'I am Nurse Brown, not Nurse Black,' cried Emma again, but Wrong John said, 'What's in a name? She's the lady all right.'

'Then ham for the lady, and a round of applause.'

Emma heard the applause, but she did not see the ham, she was too near furious tears, but the ham none the less weighed her down, and coming straight from the refrigerator it was uncomfortably cold against her chest, not to mention the wet mark it was leaving on her dress, and there was only one place she wished it.

On Dr Harding's head.

CHAPTER SEVEN

But Emma did not heave it, of course. For one thing disharmony in EC would not have looked good for the cause, for another thing Wrong John had smartly disappeared.

The wet mark on her dress did not disappear, though, and Lorraine helpfully said it probably would not. 'Brine, Emma, it rots material right through.'

'If you'd hold the ham a moment while I mop up—'

'Not me, darling, I'm not going to ruin my dress. No, Nurse, it's your baby.' Lorraine giggled at that, for anything less like a baby, though the ham because of its size had to be cradled, would have been hard to imagine.

'What am I going to do with it?' despaired Emma after she had put it down three times and three times had it returned to her.

The hall was emptying rapidly, for tomorrow was a working day and this was one job when you could not turn up half asleep. Mr Harding . . . and the rose . . . had gone. As far as the pine thicket, thought Emma bleakly, the moon buttering the dark ground beneath the leaves to a soft primrose while she, Nurse Brown, stood clutching a bare pink leg?

The trouble, too, was that the leg was becoming less pink every minute, getting a grey, second-hand look. No wonder she couldn't even give it away.

Though she did, finally—to the hospital carpenter. He said he would see to it for her, though whether this meant he would take it home to his wife or to the incinerator he did not make clear. As she climbed up to

bed a sudden thought struck Emma. What if he forgot
and put it with his tools, then left his tools out as he had
that time when old Beniston had tried to saw down the
legs of his bed, then what if old Beniston discovered it as
he had discovered the saw and took it into his cot, or did
something similarly outrageous with it? Well . . . grinning . . . it was out of her province now. Beniston could
do what he liked as far as she was concerned, infuriate
whoever he liked, but she only hoped it was Lorraine.

'You finally lost the body,' Lorraine commented as
Emma strolled down the nurses' hall.

'Yes, dear.'

Lorraine looked at her suspiciously, for Emma wore
an almost beatific look—and why not? She was thinking
pleasantly of Lorraine turning down Beniston's bed . . .
she had been transferred to seven . . . to find a bare grey
leg. The prospect delighted her.

'I bet,' said Lorraine indignantly, 'you sold that ham
and pocketed the cash. You and your cause!'

The next morning Emma took one look at the formidable spillover into the street from EC and felt like
spilling away herself. It must have been the Closed Day
yesterday that did it, closed for public patients, only
open for those sent on from GPs, for the Black Hole was
like an ants' nest.

She crawled in by the back way and made at once for
the seating. This was something she knew without being
told would have to be done.

Again she went over the patter; everyone to sit in the
rotation of their tickets. Wouldn't they ever learn? Then
she remembered that today's would be a different batch
of people from the other days, so how could they know,
poor dears? Her eye ran along the almost endless queue,
or so it seemed, and she thought sadly how many people
needed attention for that most precious gift of all, sight.

If I can help, she resolved, feeling dedicated again, then I'll gladly do it, even if it is just a humble task like this. Spurred on, she bullied the in-patients into their rows, then spinning around, still unbidden, she collected the eye exercise class.

She sat them down, instructed the parents to take note for their children, then began the orthoptic training. It went so smoothly that she felt her enthusiasm becoming a little less fevered. To be really on your toes you needed setbacks, she thought. Which reminded her that Eye Exercise Setback Number One was not present. Where was Malcolm, she wondered, of the crossed eyes and the 'mucky rot'?

'Palm,' she instructed, and showed her class how to. When they did, she tiptoed out to Sister Morrow.

Sister Morrow was pleased with her and said so briefly. 'You've caught on, Nurse, you just bogged in this morning like an old hand.'

'But not on Malcolm. Where is Malcolm? Recovered so soon? That speaks well for orthoptics.'

'Malcolm is up in the ward, and that's what I came along for, Nurse. You seem to have everything in control here, so you can go upstairs for an hour.'

'Doing what?' asked Emma.

'If I spoke from my heart I'd say doing in Malcolm,' admitted Sister aggrievedly. 'That boy!'

'Is he in for an operation?'

'No, a detailed examination, but several hours prior to the examination his eyes have to be bound. I've bound them'—Sister's voice was grim—'but I haven't bound him. I think now I should.' She rubbed her leg painfully. 'Of course,' she admitted fairly, 'under the circumstances I suppose the child couldn't see.'

'Couldn't see what?'

'You'll find out.' Sister Morrow bustled off.

Emma dismissed the orthoptics class and climbed the same stairs that last night she had climbed ahead of Wrong John. Where was Dr Harding this morning? Had he visited Greg of the little white cataracts? She wondered if Greg was still in, and the donor eye case, the tear duct, but she didn't wonder for long, instead she suffered, for the next minute she was yelping, 'Ouch!'.

It was Malcolm, his eyes bound up, but, as Sister had said, not bound up himself. On the contrary, he was careering along on three wheels, on the hospital's small tricycle placed there for little patients, and if it had not been that he couldn't see, unfortunate lad, Emma would have given him back what he gave her, two bruised shins.

As it was she contented herself with reproaching, 'Watch where you're going, Malcolm.'

'Can't,' reproached Malcolm in his turn, and he put pathos into his voice.

'Of course.' Emma was ashamed. 'Just don't bump into people, dear, it hurts.'

'No,' said Malcolm, and veered straight at Emma again and inflicted two more bruises, the knees this time.

'Malcolm!' Emma called at a third attack. 'I just don't believe you can't see.'

'All right,' challenged Malcolm, 'try it yourself.' His hands went up to his eyes.

'Don't you dare take off your bandage,' warned Emma.

'Then put one of your own on and try to see,' muttered Malcolm in further challenge, his bottom lip protruding so that it almost reached up to the bandage.

'Well, I just will,' accepted Emma grimly, and she went purposefully to the cupboard and took out the wherewithal. She'd show him!

'I'll tie it,' offered Malcolm, and Emma knelt down and submitted to darkness, wondering suspiciously as Malcolm tied her up how he could tie so that everything was completely obscured when, according to him, he couldn't see himself.

'Malcolm, you're a fraud, and it won't do you a bit of good because you'll have to undergo being bound up all over again. For two hours before the examination, Doctor says . . . Malcolm . . . Malcolm . . . *Malcolm!*' Her voice rang in emptiness, you could always tell emptiness even when you could not see it. 'Malcolm, you infuriating child, come back and unbind me at once, and tell me at the same time how you could see to tie knots if you were as black as I am now.'

Black . . . Blackie . . . That was what Wrong John called her, and if Wrong John came up the stairs and found her like this he'd have a lot more to say. It was no use her trying to edge the bandage off here, it was too public; she must grope her way into some corner and try to do it, some place where she would not be seen, where she would not be made a laughing stock of as, and let's face it, Emma, she richly deserved. But just wait, she fumed, just you wait, Malcolm my boy.

Gingerly she edged forward. Awful if the next step took her to the top of the stairs and she fell down. But it didn't, thank heaven, instead it took her to a button; it felt like a button, a man's coat button. So Wrong John had climbed up to sneer . . .

'All right,' she invited thickly, 'laugh!'

When he did not do so she invited further, 'Split your sides laughing, burst that button that's poking into me—go on, guffaw!'

Still silence, and then at last, apologetically, 'If I burst a button it would mean sewing it back again, Nurse, and just now I haven't the time.'

There was no mistaking that voice, gentle yet firm, cool yet full of warmth, considerate, wise, quite uncensorious, never Wrong John's, but *Right* John's. Mr Harding's voice.

'Oh, I'm sorry, I'm terribly sorry, sir. I—I'm bound up.'

'So I see, Nurse.'

'I suspected Malcolm . . . he was bruising shins, he even bruised Sister's, also my knees.'

'Go on, Nurse.'

'I suspected he wasn't as bound up as he said, so to prove he was fibbing I let him—well, I let him—' A long pause. 'I was an idiot,' admitted Emma. As there was no comment, and had she been able to see then Emma would have known *why*, for the great Mr Harding was literally doubled up with laughter, Emma concluded pathetically, 'Now I can't untie myself.'

'This rather puts you at a disadvantage.' John Harding had found words at last. He was looking at the tendrils of red curls tumbling over the white bandage. So bright, so flag bright, he thought.

'Here, let me unfasten you, Nurse.' His voice was a little terse with sudden emotion.

Emma took the terseness for a reprimand, and why not, she deserved the worst.

But the face that met her blink after the darkness was dissolved was as gentle as the untying hands had been; Mr Harding even smiled at her as the bandage was unrolled.

'What conclusion did you reach, Nurse?'

'Conclusion?' she echoed.

'Was Malcolm deliberately inflicting those wounds?'

'Well,' admitted Emma, 'had I been on a tricycle just now I certainly would have inflicted a few myself, but I still have my doubts about Malcolm. He could have steered at me deliberately. I mean, if he couldn't see at all how did he tie me up?'

'That's a question he will probably not answer, but I have my way of finding out. Malcolm! Malcolm!'

'Yes, sir.' Though Emma knew she could have called all day and got no result, now the small boy came out at once.

'We're taking off your bandage, Malcolm.' As he said it John Harding's deft fingers got to work again.

When the child was unbandaged he sat him down on a chair and looked lengthily into each eye in turn.

'You've been cheating, Malcolm,' he said at length.

'No, sir. Cross my heart, sir. Oh, all right, yes, sir.'

'Why?'

'Because it was too dark underneath it, so I wriggled it a bit so I could see. I don't mind if it's not all dark, I just hate black.' Malcolm's voice drooped.

'I've explained to you, Malcolm, that if you don't do what we tell you to it will be *very* black *very* much longer, and you'd hate that.'

'Yes, sir.'

'I also think that rather than hate the dark on this occasion you wanted to have a little lark, Malcolm, drive into people yet get away with it, pretend you couldn't see.'

'I couldn't see. Well, only a little bit.'

'And that little bit has undone our experiment, spoiled the whole thing. I'm sorry, Malcolm, but you'll have to start all over again. This time *I* will bandage you, bandage you very firmly, and Nurse will sit beside you to watch.'

'Oh, sir!'

He looked so disconsolate that Emma said, 'I'll read to you.'

'Eye exercises,' Malcolm commented gloomily, 'that mucky rot.'

'No, *Treasure Island*.' Emma had glimpsed the small row of books and was rather surprised at books in an eye ward, though she supposed they were here to be read to patients, not for the patients to read for themselves.

Malcolm submitted to lying down, and Emma settled herself beside him and began to read. Mr Harding had crossed over to the eye donor case, drawn the screen and shaded the light.

He was there a long time, so long that Emma had read quite a few pages by the time he emerged.

He crossed to stand by Malcolm's cot and look down at the small boy, very vulnerable and rather angelic in bed, not a shin-bruiser any more. He waited several minutes, then held up his hand for Emma to stop reading. She did so, but there was no protest from Malcolm.

'As I thought,' said Mr Harding, 'he's asleep.'

'On *Treasure Island*? We were up to an exciting part.'

'There was a relaxing tablet before that first bandage. Sister Morrow gave it, and it would have acted much sooner had Malcolm permitted it.' Mr Harding smiled and touched the little brown head. 'Now it's caught up.'

'What is wrong with Malcolm, sir?'

'It would take me longer than the time I have available to tell you right now, Nurse, but it's a fairly serious matter.'

'Poor little boy!'

'You can actually say that of a tyrant who rewards you with a bruised shin, who interrupts your orthoptic class with the continual comment of "Mucky rot"? Oh, yes, I've heard about that.'

Emma smiled back at him, and he said, 'Could you bear some more of the same sort of rot from me?'

'Sir?'

'I'm just leaving to give a short lecture, Nurse, I would like to say in our lecture room, but actually it's in the hat and cloak cupboard. The eye donor case is all right, Gregory is downstairs, the tear duct has gone and Malcolm will sleep most of his two hours. Well?' He smiled.

Emma was on her feet, *Treasure Island* forgotten. Here, her heart was exulting, was all the treasure she could ask.

'Thank you, sir,' she accepted, and followed Mr Harding down the stairs.

A little group from Southern Star up the hill had gathered in the lecture room that was really the hat and cloak cupboard. There was no room for chairs, and, by the time the lecturer . . . and Emma . . . came in, little room for standing. But room had to be made for the speaker, of course, and as Mr Harding passed through the deferential little gathering he took Emma with him.

'Wait there, Nurse,' he instructed, oblivious, though Emma wasn't, of the glare of the person whose position Emma had usurped. It happened to be Dr Harding, Wrong John, so instead of feeling apologetic Emma felt victorious.

Mr Harding had climbed on to a small ladder and he began at once.

'Because of the inconvenience you are all suffering I will not attempt to make this official; I can still remember my own crowded days, when I often had to write my notes against a fellow student's back.'

'Was it as bad then?' disbelieved someone in a very congested row.

'It wasn't much better. However, when we have our new premises, our brand-new lecture hall and desks, we will forget all this.' He swept an arm round the room, including one of the student doctors balancing on a hat rack. 'Just as well,' he smiled, 'there will be no attempt to note-take today.'

'What is on the programme, sir?'

'Just a few elementary facts at this juncture. Next lecture we will borrow space from hospital proper.'

'This is hospital proper.' Emma spoke before she thought, spoke pridefully, and she reddened, but Mr Harding only rewarded her with a grateful smile.

'Thank you, Nurse.'

At the side of her Wrong John hissed, 'Sucker!'

'Because we are more or less an unadvanced class'— Mr Harding looked apologetically at the gathering—'not advanced, anyway, in this particular medical field, these initial few words will be very elemental. And'—with feeling for them, for they were indeed very squashed—'brief.

'I thought I would talk on what brings people to us. Simply, and in a layman term: "Eye-strain." Otherwise, eye discomfort.'

'Which has nothing on discomfort,' grumbled Wrong John in Emma's ear, 'to the rib. Keep your damned elbow to yourself, Black.'

Emma retaliated by sharpening her elbow into his stomach.

'Ouch!' protested Wrong John.

'Yes, Doctor?' inquired Mr Harding.

'This eye discomfort,' asked Wrong John promptly, his foot coming to rest intentionally on Emma's and pinning it down so she could not move, 'is it regardless of age?'

'Most symptoms occur in early middle age when people first of all discover they need reading glasses. But "eye-strain" as illustrated by headaches, red, gritty, aching or tired eyes occurs at any stage of life.'

'So does murder,' whispered Wrong John, as Emma, having edged out her foot, began her elbow attack again.

'This particular instance of age will be appreciated by you housemen,' continued Mr Harding, 'especially since its basis has nothing to do with my own branch. Mary, ten, according to her mother, has strained her eyes watching TV as she always sits too close to the screen. Examination finds something altogether different, it finds diseased tonsils, which often result in red, scaly lids.'

'*I* am red and scaled,' suffered Wrong John. He impressed Emma's foot again, firmer this time.

'Another instance,' said Mr Harding. 'We will take Marion.'

'I won't,' mumbled Wrong John, 'I've had enough of women.'

'Aged sixteen, starting office work, and after a few months complains that she develops headaches every afternoon. Finds reading glasses do not help, so consults ophthalmic surgeon. Although she is slightly long-sighted, glasses are discouraged, and orthoptics recommended instead. Perhaps'—Mr Harding smiled across at Emma—'Nurse will say a few words.'

Emma started to blurt, 'But, Mr Harding, I couldn't,' met the calm, kind gaze, and found she could instead.

She went through the patter she gave to her orthoptic class, and was amazed and rather elated at how well she remembered it.

'Thank you, Nurse,' said Mr Harding when she had done. 'So much for Marion. At the end of three weeks she had lost her headache. Now we take Paul Smith.'

'Thank heaven for a male,' muttered Wrong John.

'Aged fifty, has noticed for the past few months gritty eyes at the end of the day. On questioning he says he also notices haloes sometimes around lights. As a result of several tests the specialist discovers that Mr Smith has raised pressure in the eyeballs—a disease called glaucoma. This disease affects about three people in every hundred over forty years, and, unhappily, is one of the major causes of blindness. Diagnosed early, drops will bring pressure back to normal; otherwise surgery is required. If treatment is delayed, glaucoma will permanently damage the optic nerve and cause blindness.

'In Paul Smith's case the specialist started the desired eye-drops and a week later the pressure was normal.'

Wrong John was moving forward, but it was not to inflict more pressure, Emma saw, it was in interest.

'Eye-drops, sir,' he asked, 'are they always desirable?'

'If the eyes are clear and comfortable, as normal healthy eyes should be, it is not desirable to bathe them with lotions. However, if the patient is working in a dusty atmosphere, and the eyes become red by the end of the day, they may be bathed in some simple sterile solution such as cooled bicarbonate of soda. The use of decongestion drops as a cosmetic is safe, but not advised after forty.'

'Take note, Nurse,' said Wrong John softly.

'Foreign bodies,' called a voice at the back of the hat cupboard.

'A drop of castor or paraffin oil will make the eye more comfortable than rubbing it, or pulling the upper lid over the lower will often dislodge what shouldn't be there. Both of these treatments of course,' added Mr Harding, 'are failing proper medical care. In short, to be passed on *to* the patient for his own use.' He paused. 'Any more questions?'

'Yes,' softly from Wrong John. 'How to remove an elbow out of your—'

'It's not! I mean, I can't help it. If you were standing here—' began Emma.

'Then I would be nearer to Mr Harding, wouldn't I?'

'Is that what's troubling you? Are you jealous?'

'Of you?'

'They were your words.'

'Good lord, perish the thought. Please, Nurse, could you remove that elbow long enough for me to clap?'

For Mr Harding was leaving now, the gathering making a small passage for him to pass through, and, typical of the great man, when he reached Emma he included her in the easiest exit.

While the others squashed up, Mr Harding and Emma walked out of the room like a king and queen, a state of affairs that pleased Emma so much that as she left Dr Harding she firmly implanted *her* foot on Wrong John's. She was not his weight, so what she lacked in substance she made good by a thorough grinding in.

To the resultant 'Ouch!' she glided victoriously out.

CHAPTER EIGHT

SISTER Morrow was coping along in the surgery with an eye that did not need its owner to announce that it was sore. It was very swollen, very red, very watery.

To Mr Harding's kindly inquiry as to what was wrong the sufferer said bitterly, 'Bung eye.' He added, 'I know you can see that, but it's all I can tell you. It just came up for no reason at all.'

Mr Harding examined it at length. Seeing Emma still by his side, and obviously very interested, he explained for both the nurse and the patient, 'I'm looking for a small stye or a tiny kick among the lashes that might have caused this.' He searched for some minutes, but unsuccessfully. 'There doesn't appear to be anything.'

'And I don't feel there is anything,' grieved the patient. 'I mean, you usually have a drawn-up sensation with a stye, and I just feel—feel—'

'Yes?' encouraged Right John.

'Bunged up.'

Emma half smiled at Mr Harding, but he was peering closely at some little marks near the man's hairline, around the forehead.

'What were you doing last week-end?' he asked companionably.

The patient looked surprised, but said, 'Gardening. This weather the weeds fairly leap up.'

'And so do midges on certain weeds,' nodded Mr Harding. He turned to Emma. 'Take note, Nurse, another hazard of spring; beside the lawn-mower incidents there will undoubtedly be some of these "bung eyes".'

'You mean I've been bitten, Doctor?' asked the patient.

'Obviously the harvest, or red-backed midge, has been at your forehead, and I believe one has descended on the lid of your eye.'

'I never saw anything.'

'They're very minute, you would need a glass. Even then they could pass for a dust speck.'

'A little thing like that could cause an eye like this!'

'It has, hasn't it? But don't worry, it will probably settle down quite smartly. Take this along to the dispensary and you'll be told what to do.'

When the 'bung eye' had gone Mr Harding added, 'The eye would settle down without any treatment, but the soothing solution he'll be given will make him feel better about it.' He paused. 'I'm going up to unbind our young enemy now, so you can come and help me, Nurse.'

Emma went readily, hoping to vindicate herself this time, to really be some help with Malcolm.

The boy was still in the cot, though no longer asleep. He was nicely pliable, though, after the sedation, and submitted amiably to being unbandaged and examined.

Mr Harding took out the ophthalmoscope that he carried as other doctors carry stethoscopes and peered into Malcom's eyes.

'The retina and other parts of the eye can be examined, Nurse,' he explained, 'by throwing a beam of light where it is needed, and by different lenses being interposed.'

'What can you see?' Emma and Malcolm said together.

Mr Harding answered Malcolm first. 'A little pig in a sty that's starting on the bottom lid in the left eye and a wink in the right.'

To Emma he said, 'An image of the fundus, which is the retina and optic nerve.' He added quietly, 'I'll talk about it some other time.'

Malcolm asked with interest, 'Can you really see a wink? What's a wink like? I mean I know it goes like this, but what's it like?'

'You go downstairs with Nurse and she'll tell you,' directed Mr Harding. 'Take him, please,' he said to Emma. 'I'm going to spend a little time with my donor case again.'

Emma understood at once, she knew any small boy, let alone Malcolm, would not be needed. 'Come along, Malcolm,' she said firmly.

Malcolm went unwillingly. He would sooner have stayed upstairs where the tricycle was, and other toys, from where, Emma suspected, he could lean over the banisters and drop things on unsuspecting heads.

That this had actually been in Malcolm's mind was proved by the fluffy duster he found time to throw over before they descended, the recipient below, a little old lady, letting out a squeal. Emma could not help wishing it had been Alf Croker, and the duster to him some form of delirium tremens, whereupon, discouraged at last from attending EC, he took off. She felt the Eye Clinic could have done without its Alfred Croker.

'*Come along*, Malcolm!'

'Can I slide down?'

'Of course not.'

'Can I jump?'

'No, you can't.'

'Two steps at a time?'

'Oh, all right.' Anything to silence him, decided Emma.

But Malcolm was not silenced. 'What colour was that wink the doctor saw in my eye?'

'Pink.'

'Dark pink or light pink?'

'Striped.'

'As well as a grinder of adult insteps,' put in a voice beside her, 'you're a liar to little children. Pink winks! Also,' asked Wrong John, 'where have you been?'

'It's nothing to do with you, but I'll tell you: assisting Mr Harding.'

'You assisting him? A half-fledged black-legs?'

'Assisting him with an eye injury,' said Emma proudly, forbearing to add that it had been a 'bung eye.' 'Assiting him with Malcolm,' she added, 'while he was examined through the ophthalmoscope.'

'My, my, what big words we're up to!'

'And where were you?' finished Emma.

'Having my foot attended to,' answered Wrong John with feeling.

'I hope it's bruised.'

'It's broken.'

'Good!'

Malcolm was looking delightedly from one to the other. This was better than throwing things from upstairs.

Emma took him firmly by the hand and along the passage to where Sister Morrow put her to feeding in-patients to Mr Harding, who would soon return from his donor case and would be working on his day's tally again.

'You can keep Malcolm by you,' directed Sister. 'It'll be safer than returning him upstairs.'

'Is he stopping in, then?'

'For several days, anyway until Mr Harding makes up his mind about an operation. His parents work, so we can't send him home. Apart from the impending op he has a few more examinations yet, and by the look of business'—Sister glanced despairingly along the queue—'those examinations will have to be fitted in whenever there's a spare moment.'

Emma, having begun the flow in to the specialist by this time, asked, 'Is Malcolm likely to take off?' She had visions of chasing him as she had chased the girl in pink, but she knew that in Malcolm's case it would be a longer, harder chase.

'Not a chance,' answered Sister. 'He's like our Alf Croker, an Old Man, juvenile variety, of the Sea. No, Malcolm finds the Eye Clinic a much more interesting place than Basket Lane where he lives: also, though you and I might not rave over the ham sandwiches, here to Malcolm they comprise beaut grub.'

'Is he neglected?'

'I would say superfluous. He has nine brothers and sisters, so ham would not be on the menu.'

'But love would?' Emma asked anxiously, for in spite of Malcolm being a wicked little boy she had a soft spot for him.

Sister shrugged. 'The rest of the family have normal sight,' she said.

'That would make the one who hasn't mean all the more.'

'Not after you've fetched or arranged to have him fetched for treatment for nine months.'

'Is it that long?'

'Yes, and apparently it loses its novelty. Malcolm lately comes alone.' Sister bit back a sigh, her glance flicking to the hazardous street outside EC portals. 'Don't be too hard on our bruiser,' she said.

Malcolm was moving among the rows. He was a cunning little piece, he seemed to sense a goody in a paper bag even before the bag emerged and the paper crackled. He knew to a nicety when the goodies were depleted and when to move to another possible source. Emma supposed you had to have such knowledge when you were one of ten.

'Number Twelve,' she called.

Twelve was a young man in a seaman's uniform, and he looked confused and unhappy. Another young seaman with him said to Emma, 'He's a froggy and doesn't understand a word, so I came with him.'

'Does he understand you?'

'No, miss.'

'Then what's the use of you coming?'

'To show him where. I came here when I got a piece of metal removed from my eye. They took it out with an electro-magnet.' The young seaman was all ready to describe the operation, so Emma got in first.

'Has *he* metal in his eye?' she inquired.

'Dunno what he has, he's a froggy.'

'But couldn't you have taken him to the ship's doctor?'

'Our tub's not big enough to carry an MO. Besides, everyone knows it's here you come for your eyes. And eyes it is, you can see that for yourself.'

Emma could see . . . the boy's eyes were inflamed and red.

'Is yours a French ship?'

'I'm no froggy . . . no, we picked Pierre up in New Caledonia, we called in on our way home. He's the only Frenchie who signed on.'

'Is his name really Pierre?'

'I call him that. Can I beetle off now and collect him later? I haven't much liberty you see, and I picked up some French *parfum . . . parfum* is scent, Nurse . . . in Noumea, and I want to give it to my best girl—you understand.'

'Next, please, Nurse,' Mr Harding called patiently, and Emma said, 'All right' to the delivering seaman, and to the young Frenchman, '*Suivez-moi, s'il vous plaît.*'— 'Please follow me.'

Pierre, or whatever his name was, looked up eagerly, and Mr Harding did, too, as Emma said next, '*Asseyez-vous ici, s'il vous plaît.*'—'Sit here, please.'

'You've been hiding your light, Nurse,' Mr Harding commended as he took up his ophthalmoscope. 'Next time a foreign patient comes without an interpreter we won't need to wait until we can bring one in.'

'It'll have to be a French patient, then,' admitted Emma humbly, yet pleased with herself for all her humility. 'French, I'm afraid, is all I have, and in Australia we don't have many French patients.'

'Well, your French is going to be useful now. May I ask where you learned it, Nurse?'

'Fortunately, as regards accent, from the same island from which our patient comes. My father was stationed in Noumea when I was a child.'

'Excellent,' smiled Mr Harding, and Emma's heart sang. It was soul-satisfying, she thought, to please this man.

Mr Harding took a long time in his examination, keeping Emma by him to question the patient and relay back the answers.

In the middle of the procedure Dr Harding came in, and it gave Emma more satisfaction still to keep him waiting, obviously, though unwillingly, not unimpressed by what he heard, while she rattled off in his native language to the young seaman.

Wrong John turned a little fractiously to leave again,

but Mr Harding called him back.

'This is of interest, Doctor. Here we have a probable obstruction of the lachrymal duct, and I suspect a swelling, or even an abscess, has collected between the nose and eye.'

At once Wrong John lost his fractiousness and in his interest forgot all about Emma and her French. He peered, too, at Pierre, and he and Mr Harding spoke quietly together.

At length Mr Harding told Emma to ask Pierre whether he would need to return to his ship before he was placed in hospital.

The boy looked alarmed, and Emma soothed him by saying it would be just for an examination.

'It won't be, though,' put in Mr Harding. 'Oh, yes, Nurse, I can follow if not converse. No, this lad needs not an eye specialist but a nose man. The defect is not a grave one, and it can be treated, but it will take longer than just an examination, and it will have to be done up the hill, not here. Can you tell him that as kindly as possible?'

Emma told him . . . told him that his friend would be informed and would inform the ship . . . that everything would be all right and not to worry.

Slowly the boy's face lightened.

'Good, Nurse, very good. And now perhaps you could conduct him up to Southern Star. You go, too, Doctor, to explain to Admission.'

In the end four of them went. Malcolm, of course, had to tag on.

'I can speak French,' Malcolm boasted. 'I can say parleyvoo.'

The young seaman, impressed with the bigger hospital, obviously much happier now, smiled back at Malcolm and said accommodatingly, '*Parlez vous.*'

While Dr Harding arranged admission, Emma, who had intended to hurry back to EC—and Mr Harding's side—chased up Malcolm. She found him in the canteen, his nose flattened against the glass display as he gazed at a pink cake.

'Come along, Malcolm.'

Malcolm did not hear.

'Malcolm, *come at once!*'

'Give the kid a go,' broke in Dr Harding at Emma's side, 'or do you only allot favours to older males?'

'Meaning?' asked Emma, irritated. She added, 'I have to get back to work.'

'That should be "I have to get back to the great John Harding." Thanks, miss, two coffees and a raspberry pop.'

'Coke,' preferred Malcolm.

'We'll have to go,' fretted Emma.

'We can't—yet. They're admitting Pierre, but will need you in fifteen minutes for some more translation. My, my, how you enjoyed your moments today, Nurse.' The coffee had come and Wrong John was offering her the sugar. 'Sucking up beautifully, weren't you, Blackie?'

'I happen to know the language.'

'For which you're very grateful.'

'Of course I'm grateful. Couldn't I help poor Pierre?'

'He wouldn't have died.'

'I can't understand you . . . Malcolm, not another straw . . . anyone would think I enjoyed what I did.'

'Well, you did, didn't you?'

Emma did not reply. Yes, I enjoyed it, she was thinking secretly, I enjoyed Mr Harding's deference, his—his dependence on me, it was a very precious thing.

'You also,' put in Wrong John shrewdly, 'enjoyed topping me.'

'How ridiculous you are! You never entered my thoughts.'

'You know what, Black, I believe I entered your thoughts more than Mr Harding did. Victory is stronger than satisfaction, Nurse.' Wrong John stirred his coffee so rapidly that it spilled over. Evidently considering this something on the debit side for Dr Harding so possibly something on the credit side for Malcolm, Malcolm observed promptly, 'You're slopping,' and followed it up with, 'Can I have a pink cake?'

'Why do you go on so childishly?' demanded Emma of Wrong John.

'I always like a good stir of my coffee. Three pink cakes, miss.'

'None for me, and you know I didn't mean the coffee.'

'No, you meant Mr Harding.'

'I did. You go on as though—as though—' Emma flushed.

'As though I'm jealous of him? You've said that before. Well, I am. To have knowledge, to have instinct, even to have hands like he has.' Wrong John's eyes dreamed. 'But you, Black,' and his eyes gleamed now as he came back to earth, 'didn't mean that. You meant jealousy of a different strain, jealousy of him because you seek him first, and in that I bow out. You mean nothing to me, nothing at all.' He said it with a hateful smirk.

Malcolm, his mouth full of cake, asked hopefully, 'Are you two going to fight again?'

'Tooth and nail,' promised Wrong John, 'hair out by the roots.'

'Don't be a fool,' fumed Emma.

'No, don't *you* be, Blackie.' All at once Wrong John's voice was sober. 'To part is to die a little, and you are too young and red-haired for even a small death.'

She understood what he meant, though she would not have admitted it. He meant that inevitably she would be transferred from EC back to the normal hospital, or go to some other hospital, and the parting would be to die a little, a small death.

But it need not be parting, not necessarily. Emma's heart was repeating hopefully; sometimes things happened, sometimes—

'Not in this case, Black.'—Oh, why did this wretched man always have to read her thoughts? 'You see, Nurse—'

'I don't see, and I don't want to listen to you.'

He pondered over that, then inclined his head. 'No, come to think of it there's nothing I can really tell you,' he admitted, 'except—except—well, don't build, kiddo, simply *don't*. To part, remember, is to die a little,' he said again.

'Then I'm dying a little now.' Emma got up angrily. 'This is where we part. Come, Malcolm.'

'Malcolm can eat your pink cake first, the one you're frightened to eat because of your figure.'

'I have no figure troubles.'

'Ever looked in a back mirror?'

'How dare you!'

'When,' asked Malcolm, his mouth full, 'will the hair get pulled out?'

'Not this time, lad. Nurse is going to do some translating, and you and I are returning to EC.'

'Can I have some more cake?'

'You can have a kick in the pants.'

'Nice bedside manner.' Emma was moving off.

'I have,' Wrong John called impudently after her, 'other varieties.'

'So has a popular brand of sauce.'

Malcolm interrupted, 'I love termarter sauce.'

'And that's it,' indicated Wrong John of Emma. 'Red hair and much sauce.'

'It's ginger,' argued Malcolm. Then he said, for he was a lean hungry little boy, 'I love ginger beer. Do you think—'

'No, I don't. I think we're going back right now. See you later, Nurse. And remember: To part is to—'

'Die a little.' Emma stamped off—but not before she advised loathingly, 'So drop dead.'

CHAPTER NINE

EMMA went several times to the ward to visit Pierre, for Pierre, it happened, really was his name.

The young seaman was disconsolate and very homesick. He had left Noumea because he was tired of island life, he related sadly, and because everyone had said that Sydney was gay and friendly. Pierre had looked resentfully round the white walls, at the prim (during duty hours) blue-and-white-striped, starchy girls.

Emma had not tried to stir him out of his doldrums, instead she had spoken of the Noumea she remembered. The reef the incoming ships had to negotiate, the crowds waiting on the wharf, French, Japanese, Javanese, Chinese. The 'boys' who unloaded the cargo and who were always ready to break into hilarious gusts of laughter—Though she should not have said that, she thought at once, for certainly poor Pierre did not look ready to break into laughter.

His eyes gleamed, though, when he reassured her in his turn that eleven o'clock in the morning at Noumea still meant island coffee and rolls spread with guava jelly. Emma was silent for a moment as she remembered back. How delicious that guava jelly! She determined on her next day off to track some down and with it try to coax a small smile at least out of sad Pierre.

The hospital canteen had none, neither did the corner store. The only place would be some supermarket dealing in imported as well as local goodies, so when Sister Morrow said unexpectedly that afternoon that, business being a degree less pressing, and Nurse having been a good girl—Sister's actual words—Nurse could have an hour or so off, Emma agreed eagerly, even though Mr Harding was busy on in-patients, a state of affairs that prior to Pierre would have kept Emma, time off or time on, rooted to the ushering-in door. It was still cause for a wistful glance back, but Pierre, and the guava jelly, won, and Emma set off for town.

The jelly proved hard to find. All other varieties were offered to Emma with the assurance that they were even more delicious, but it had to be guava, she explained, as eaten in Noumea. Eventually a variety of guava confiture was found, and though it was more golden than the pink that Emma used to spread in New Caledonia, she decided, glancing at her watch, that it would have to do.

As well as being a different colour, she observed, coming back in the bus, it was thinner, but a few hours of refrigeration should fix that.

She hurried into EC, saw to her joy that Mr Harding was in attendance, shoved the jelly temporarily into the fridge, got into her butcher stripe, white cap and black stockings again, and reported to Sister Morrow.

Sister allotted her Eye Exercises followed by Dispensary. Emma nodded impatiently when Sister gave her the old drill of agarol and how not to be persuaded by the teenagers to hand it out willy-nilly, for she had been told many times how the younger femme fatale found it a successful eye-shadow, and her attention was not on any teenager but on the maturer figure of the woman in the dispensary back row, the woman who was both thorn and rose and Wrong John's—and Right John's?— beautiful brunette. Kristin. Sitting in the very last bench.

As she doled out the boracic and golden eye ointment Emma found herself growing progressively indignant against Kristin. What right had she here if she wasn't a genuine patient? Only doctors, nursing staff, clerks, cleaners and sufferers were allowed here, and she was none of those. Yet there she sat, evidently unchallenged, for if she had been challenged surely she wouldn't still sit. It was very unlike Sister Morrow who was so meticulous in everything else, and who once had creased her brows over her, a thing, it now occurred to Emma, that Sister Morrow no longer did. Well, if Sister Morrow was remiss, she, Nurse Brown, would not be. Holding up the doling-out for a few moments, Emma walked across.

'You are waiting for a prescription?'

No answer.

'You were sent to Dispensary?'

No response.

'You—you—' Emma found that in her indignation she had run out of questions, and at that moment the thorn turned her glance back to Emma, turned it from Mr Harding's room, most definitely from Mr Harding's room, and the big soft eyes were full of tears.

Emma was so surprised she backed back to the doling out again, in her abstraction letting one of the teenagers take out a bottle of agarol. What right had the thorn to be crying apart from the fact that tears made the beautiful eyes twice as beautiful? What right had she to be here? I'll ask again, determined Emma, and this time I won't be put off. She took a step across, but it was too late, the thorn had gone.

Instead, at the end of the back row now sat Wrong John Harding, and he looked very pleased with himself.

'Your prescription slip, please,' snapped Emma, wanting to take her futility out on someone and deciding there was none better than Junior here. 'Is it lotion, ointment, or—'

'None of those, Blackie.' He answered her benignly, ignored her bad temper. 'Nor is it soothing syrup,' he grinned.

'We don't dispense that.'

'Even if you did I wouldn't need it. I don't need soothing. I'm on top of the world.'

'You're on the back seat of the dispensary, which I am now closing. Kindly move out.'

Wrong John did not stir. 'He passed this patient on to me,' he said dreamily. '"I have reached a certain conclusion," he said.'

'Who said?'

'Harding, of course.'

'Mr Harding?'

'Yes. "See what you think," he said.'

'And did you?' she asked pertly.

'Yes.' He did not notice the pertness. 'And it coincided with his finding.'

'Certainly it would coincide if you've any sense when it's a great specialist like Mr Harding.'

'*Before*,' put in Wrong John triumphantly. 'I gave my verdict first, and it turned out it was his as well. So'— coming out of his delighted trance—'how do you like your eggs cooked now?'

'I have no ham to eat with them,' reminded Emma flatly. 'Will you move along, please, I'm shutting up the dispensary.'

'Don't you want to hear about it?'

About to make a withering rejoinder, Emma paused. Even in her self-absorption, or her absorption of Right John, she could not help but catch that wistful note. Poor Junior, she thought patronisingly, he is terribly callow, but then he can't help that.

'Yes, I'll hear.'

If he caught the patronage in her voice, he made no

sign, but it was probably he hadn't heard it, he was too lit up.

'This man was down for retina surgery,' he related. 'It was thought by the first man who saw him that the retina was detached. Then His Nibs—'

'Mr Harding.'

'Yes. Mr Harding took over and reached a certain conclusion, and without telling me that conclusion first asked me to come to a conclusion, too.'

'And you coincided, of course.' Emma stifled a yawn.

'Yes. It was not what he had been referred for, instead it was a simple instance of—well, no use telling you.'

'You asked me to listen,' she said indignantly.

'Yes. And thank you, Emma.'

A little mollified, Emma said nothing.

'Mr Harding bowed out and left the treatment to me,' resumed Wrong John.

'That was nice.'

'Nice? It was marvellous. Certainly it wasn't much in the way of treatment, just a cortisone acetate in a petrolatum basis.'

'Don't bother to tell me,' reminded Emma, recovered from her temporary softening again.

'Just an ointment,' triumphed Wrong John, 'or salve.'

'Did I issue it?' asked Emma.

'Certainly not. This stuff is kept under refrigeration. It's not in a tube like the oxide of mercury. In fact when you see it in a jar you could almost take it for jam.'

'Fancy that,' tch-tched Emma, and moved down the passage to Sister Morrow again. It was not till an hour later that she thought over Wrong John's words.

'You could take it for jam,' he had said.

What sort of jam? wondered Emma, looking at the spot where her supermarket purchase had sat and now

sat no longer. More a jelly than a jam? Pink? Yellow?
The variety called—guava?

She knelt down and almost crushed herself into the
fridge. It must have been pushed to the back, she
thought desperately. Or Sister Morrow had taken it out
for an afternoon snack. Or—

Her hand closed on something and she withdrew it
triumphantly, the same shape jar, the same size. Only it
was not guava jelly, it was—

It was a yellow salve. Wrong John's cortisone acetate
in a petrolatum basis? Oh, horrors! Where, then, was
the guava jelly?

She looked again. She looked again and again and
again. Only Sister Morrow's sharp, 'Nurse, there could
be *donor eyes* in there,' brought her out of the fridge in a
rush. Sister's affronted glare said only too clearly that
had it been earlier in the day certainly Nurse would not
have been allotted an hour off. And, thought Emma
desperately, if only that had happened she would not be
in the pickle . . . pickle? no, that was the wrong preserve
. . . that she was now.

It hadn't happened, though. She actually had gone
into town and actually had bought a jar of guava jelly
that was simply not there any more. Where, oh, where
was the jelly? Was it—Could it be—Oh, no. No!

Three times Sister caught her up reproachfully for not
attending as she should. 'You might get away with it up
the hill, Nurse, but eyes are different, they demand all
your attention all the time. I can't understand you this
afternoon. Have you anything on your mind?'

'No, Sister.' (Only a jar of guava jelly.)

'Then pull yourself together, Nurse, and see to those
patients awaiting their normalising drops.'

'Yes, Sister.'

The patients did not fare well. Those whose drops did

not roll down their cheeks received them down their necks. Emma retreated before the murmurs of indignation became a loud chorus of protest and asked what else she could do.

Sister, a little mollified by her promptness, and fortunately out of range of the damp patients, said tea would not go amiss. While the water boiled Emma searched through the fridge again in the hope that the guava jelly had returned. It had not.

Though it was customary for the staff to come for their tea breaks, on this occasion Emma poured and carried a cup herself to Wrong John. He rolled his eyes at this unexpected service, and as he was eyelid feeling for primary disturbances he nodded for Emma to put the cup down. Emma did, but still lingered.

'Ahem,' she began surreptitiously.

'You spoke, Nurse?'

'I—I asked if you were finding any foreign bodies?'

'Like Sophia Loren?'

'Like—jam.'

'Jam?'

'I was just wondering what would happen if by mistake—'

'You spread your jam on your eye instead of on your bread?'

The patient belonging to the closed eyelids wriggled and Wrong John answered, 'Ants.'

'A—apart from ants?'

'Wouldn't ants be enough?'

'I mean—would—would anything happen? Anything—dangerous?'

'Depends on the make.'

'Guava.'

'What? No, not the fruit, nit, the sort, home-made or factory. Home-made would presumably use no preservative, but shop goods—'

'Would the preservative, would it—'

'Keep still, please,' Wrong John directed his patient. He directed Emma, 'Hop off.'

Emma went tremblingly back to the teapot. Preservatives!

'You're very pensive, Nurse.' Mr Harding was grabbing a cup between patients, and he raised his brows on Emma as she came in. 'Is it our Frenchman?'

'In a way,' said Emma truthfully. But for the guava jelly, she thought, and but for Pierre, this would never have happened. 'Sir'—falteringly—'preservatives—'

'Nurse?'

'Are they harmful? I mean—'

He was smiling down at her, smiling at the bright red shine of her hair. 'What do you mean, child?'

'What you put in food to keep it,' she blurted.

'I'm no chemist.' He smiled again. 'However, I don't think you need worry about what you eat of our preserved foods these days.'

'It wasn't eating,' said Emma, then fell silent, feeling a fool. How could you say that it was *applying*, applying to an *eye*?

Mr Harding put down his cup, passed his hand a little wearily over his own eyes and went back to his patients.

Just to make sure a miracle hadn't happened Emma investigated the fridge again.

The steps were on her before she could emerge and shut the door. This time Sister Morrow wouldn't let her off with a rebuke. But it wasn't Sister, it was Wrong John, and had Emma not leapt away so guiltily he might not have noticed.

'Ahah!' he pounced. 'What goes on? No wonder you fetched me tea, Blackie, with your own bottle party going on here.'

'It wasn't. You're quite absurd.' Emma stood in front of the fridge. 'I was just checking.'

'Checking what? And don't say donor eyes, because when they're in, the fridge is locked.'

'Nothing. I mean I was doing nothing.' Emma in her concern posted herself right in front of the handle now.

'Methinks the lady doth protest too much. Move aside, female, while I see the brand.'

When Emma did not move, he moved her. He did it easily, effortlessly. She always thought of him as a callow junior, not a big, effortless man. Dr Harding then looked curiously in.

'Nothing, as you protested,' he said at length in surprise, 'nothing except the usual EC collection of ocular and stomach wants, drops and milk, salve and butter. By the way, Black, this is the salve I was speaking of, the cortisone acetate in a petrolatum basis.' He closed the fridge, wearing again that pleased look that he had before. 'To think that instead of having a delicate op that fellow is instead bathing his eyes in a simple lotion followed by an application of this—this—'

He stopped. Stopped short. He looked at Emma, looked at the fridge, opened the fridge.

'How,' he asked in a frozen voice, 'if I've given a patient a jar of cortisone acetate in a petrolatum basis is it still here?'

'Because,' said Emma wretchedly, 'I think you gave him guava jelly.'

'What?'

'That—that was why I asked you about jam. You see, I'd put in some jelly. For Pierre. It—it was in a jar like this. And it was yellow—I was worried about that, in Noumea it was more of a pink.'

'When,' hissed Wrong John, 'did all this occur to your bird-brain?'

'When Pierre was so unhappy. I thought it would take him home, in spirit I mean.'

'I wish you were home, and not in spirit. I mean when did the significance of the presence of the salve and not the jelly occur to you?'

'When I came and asked you about jam.'

'And you let all that time go? Do you realise that you may have—may have—'

'Mr Harding said not to worry.'

'*You told him?*'

'No, of course not . . . at any rate not in so many words. I did ask about preservatives, but—'

Emma babbled to herself. For Wrong John—and the right salve—had gone.

The rest of the day went agonizingly slowly. Had she done some awful damage too horrible to contemplate with whatever preservative went into guava jelly, had the sugar attracted ants, had the seeds of the fruit—

'Really, Nurse, for all the good you've been today you might as well not have come to work. You can go now.'

'But, Sister—'

'I said go, not only because I've had enough of you but because tomorrow we are expecting some bed patients for the day, and you will be on duty upstairs. I hope for a little more alertness than you've shown this afternoon.'

'I'm sorry, Sister.' Emma collected her things and went out slowly. For all her self-absorption she noted that Kristin's car was parked outside EC and that in it Kristin waited for Mr Harding. It didn't anger her this time, though, she felt too worried.

When she reached the Norfolk pine thicket someone stepped out. Wrong John Harding.

'Cheer up, Nurse,' he said, 'though you don't deserve it I have to put you out of your misery. No one is dead.'

'Or blind?'

'Or anything.'

'The jelly was harmless? I mean the preservative?'

'I don't know, and I'll never know, for it no longer exists. I had tea with the Malways and we had it on toast.'

'Oh, I'm so glad!' Emma's eyes swam with relief.

'I should think Pierre would be, too, it was very poor jam.'

'Had they discovered it before you got there?'

'Yes, the kettle was on the boil.'

'But seriously—'

'*Not* seriously, Nurse,' he warned, 'for if we become serious I can tell you that you're in for a very unpleasant tongue-bang.' He looked sternly down on her. 'Taking all that time,' he drove home severely, 'to tell me what had happened.'

About to lower her eyes in shame, a truth of her own came to Emma. The truth about Dr Harding, his part in the episode.

Gleefully, triumphantly, she tossed it back at him.

'And who,' she demanded, '*issued* guava jelly instead of cortisone acetate in a petrolatum basis?'

'How could I help it,' he defended, 'placed on the shelf like that?'

'But you never looked enough, did you? You never checked, then double checked. A good doctor is careful, cautious, meticulous, painstaking, responsible, trust—'

'Oh, shut up,' said Wrong John Harding, and he turned on his heel and strode off to the sound of Emma's mirth.

The only person Emma really could feel sorry for, seeing Mr Malway as well as the cortisone acetate had scored her guava jelly, was Pierre.

But when she went to visit Pierre that night she saw she had no need any longer to be sorry.

Pierre needed no jelly. Indeed he did not need Noumea. Sydney was bright after all, Sydney was friendly. Especially with one of the prettiest, now not so prim, starchless nurses, off duty, sitting on his bed, giggling, whispering, occasionally touching his hand.

Emma murmured, '*Pardonnez moi*,' and slipped out.

CHAPTER TEN

THE next day Emma, on Sister Morrow's orders, went immediately upstairs for ward duty.

'You're a general nurse today,' called Sister after her. 'No eye drops, no forms, no exercises, no dispensary, no ushering in. I only hope you haven't forgotten all your hospital drill.'

Emma hoped so, too. Although it was only a short while since she had left the world of Beds: how to make, Food: how to prepare, Patient: how to bathe, this second world of hers, this world of eyes, either because of the excitement and intimacy of working almost shoulder to shoulder in confined quarters, of working on the most precious sense of all, sight . . . or was it working with Mr Harding? had dimmed any memory of previous progress she must have achieved.

'I only hope,' worried Emma, 'I haven't forgotten temperatures.'

But at once, getting into the swing of things, she remembered all she had learned. She supposed it was like swimming; you didn't forget.

The patients must have been admitted last night, she decided as she bustled around, so as to be ready for early ops, for they were well settled in. Moving briskly between beds, doing the many routine things she had been taught for two and a half years, Emma found herself enjoying General Hospital again. After all, she thought, shaking the mercury in the thermometer down below normal, this is why I became a nurse.

She noticed that though sedatives had evidently been

administered, pre-op tablets had not. The patients, with
the exception of the end cot who slept deeply, were
relaxed, but only mildly so, not semi-pre-anaesthetised
as was the accepted routine in the hospital up the hill,
and she supposed that this would be since their operations would necessarily call for local anaesthetic so that
they themselves could assist in the treatment they were
undergoing.

A cheerful woman in the second bed told Emma this
was so. 'To have a cyst removed from an eye,' she
smiled, 'you mustn't be asleep.'

'Is that what you're in for?'

'Yes, dear. The other cysts . . . I've had several . . .
the doctor took out while I sat up on the chair, but this
one is well under the lid.'

'Is it paining?'

'No, but it's a nuisance. I keep on trying to brush away
an eyelash that's not there at all.'

When Emma came to the last patient, the deeply
sleeping one, she could see that more than a sedative had
been given. She took up the chart and read that the
patient was to undergo general anaesthetic, so probably
the deep sleep was the result of the customary pre-
operation medication.

The cheerful cyst case again said that this was so, it
was a troublesome tear duct, so the woman had told her
last night before the medication, and as the eye itself
would not be involved, the anaesthetic would be general.

'Only she called it another name,' she related. 'I'm
afraid I can't recall.'

'The lachrymal gland,' said a kind voice, and Emma
looked up to see Mr Harding by her side.

'Good morning, Mrs Reynolds,' he smiled at the cyst
case. 'Ready to have another eyelash removed?'

'When it's you removing it, Doctor,' beamed Mrs Reynolds, 'but it's not an eyelash, is it? I just told Nurse here that that's what it feels like, but of course it isn't.'

'No, yours isn't, but occasionally an ingrowing or wrong-growing lash is the trouble.' Mr Harding turned from Mrs Reynolds to Emma. 'Good morning, Nurse.'

He looked at the deeply sleeping general anaesthetic subject, and explained quietly and lucidly to Emma. She had never been included in surgery before like this, you had to be a quite lofty sister at Southern Star to be treated in such a way, and she was thrilled.

'Do you sometimes cry, Nurse?' he questioned, then smiled at once, 'But of course you do. With your warm colouring how could I ask?'

As she looked inquiringly at him he said, 'Tears are not for the cold-hearted, and though I expect that a titian-haired subject—'

'Red.'

He persisted, 'Though a titian-haired subject could have a cool set of emotions, I would say it was generally improbable, and in you, impossible, Nurse.'

'Is—is that bad?' blurted Emma.

He looked down at her and his eyes smiled.

'Now, the lachrymal gland—' he began. 'Tears are the watery and salty fluid which moisten the eyes. They are the secretion of this lachrymal gland I spoke of, and they reach the surface of the eye by tiny ducts.'

How gentle he was, yet how strong, how grave yet how kind. Emma felt her own eyelids pricking with gratefulness for the participation he offered, and only hoped she was not going to give a practical demonstration of how the lachrymal gland worked.

'In normal circumstances there is just enough secretion poured out to keep the surface of the eyeball moist,' said Right John, 'and this is a primary function.'

Wrong John Harding had just joined them and was now standing by Emma's side. He would, she thought, he would spoil everything.

'It is essential that the cornea be kept moist in order to maintain its transparency,' said Mr Harding.

Emma's cornea felt very moist, almost as though she was going to spill over.

As though he read her fears Mr Harding said reassuringly, 'Tears are carried across the eyeball by blinking movements of the eyelids, but they are prevented from escaping over the lid margins by the oily secretion which coats there.' He smiled and included Wrong John. 'Perhaps you will go on, Doctor.'

Wrong John said academically but not nearly so beautifully or fluidly, Emma disparaged, 'Reaching the inner angle or canthus of the eye, the excess fluid passes into two tiny apertures, the puncta lachrymalia.' He gave a quick triumphant side glance at Emma.

'Quite right, Doctor,' said Mr Harding.

'These are the mouths of two fine ducts which lead into the lachrymal or tear sac,' went on Wrong John.

'And there,' put in Right John, nodding to his general anaesthetic case, 'is our trouble. The tear sacs of the two eyes lie in bony grooves, one on each side of the bridge of the nose. At their lower ends they open into the nasal ducts, and so the tears . . . those not mopped up by your handkerchief, Nurse, or a large handkerchief borrowed from your escort, for that's what happens in romantic novels, I believe . . . finally reach the nose.'

'And are blown out,' said Wrong John unromantically. *He* would!

'Now you can appreciate the importance of tears,' said Mr Harding, 'and why Mrs'—he took up the general anaesthetic's chart—'Mrs Wilson's lachrymal gland is of concern to her and to us.' In his usual generous way he included Wrong John, and Emma could almost see Wrong John swelling with pride. Well, hadn't she done the same herself?

'I won't burden you with details, Nurse, I just felt I'd like you to understand why Mrs Wilson will have a full anaesthetic yet on the other hand Mrs Reynolds during her process will probably chatter her head off as usual'— he smiled at Mrs Reynolds, who had been listening with interest to the explanation of her ward mate, and who said at once, 'Oh, Doctor, do I?'

'No, as a matter of fact you're an excellent patient.' He put down the general anaesthetic's chart again.

'Ordinarily, Nurse, we would give Mrs Wilson to the hospital up the hill to do, but in her case there are several other ocular things on which I wish to satisfy myself. so we are doing her here.'

'Is it grave?'

With the kindliest, gentlest of reproofs Right John said, 'All operations are grave, but I understand what you mean, Nurse. No, it is not a matter of gravity as we consider gravity. In fact, with the services of an anaesthetist from the hospital, Doctor'—he nodded to Wrong John—'and I will be able to cope. With, of course, your help.'

'My help?' Emma was startled. 'I—I—'

'Don't fret, child, you won't be asked to do anything you feel incapable of doing.'

'In other words,' interpreted Wrong John, as Mr Harding moved off to speak with his 'local' patients, 'help wash up, help put out clean towels, help hand out gloves, all the elementary stuff.' He looked her critically up and down. 'Did you get that far?'

'Past that,' Emma flashed back, 'even up to breaking the sad news to bereaved relatives after fledgling doctors had tried themselves out.'

'Ah,' pounced Wrong John, 'but today you have no fears, have you? Isn't the great Harding on deck, though that's not what you call him. I hear tell it's Right John, the Right John, and I'm the Wrong. Right?'

'Right,' Emma concurred, and moved across to accompany the specialist on his rounds.

There were two other cysts to be removed, a proptosis, or prominence, Mr Harding interpreted, to be examined more thoroughly under mild sedation, and a pteryguim, or fleshy growth in the conjunctiva, to receive operative treatment.

'Usually we don't interfere,' Right John said of the fleshy growth, 'but, like Mrs Reynolds' eyelash that isn't there, it's becoming a nuisance.'

He said a few encouraging words to the final patient, then asked Emma if she would see to things in the small room that was all that temporary EC could offer for an operating theatre.

Almost bursting with pride, feeling, because of his trust in her, that she would not forget the smallest detail she had been taught, Emma said 'Yes,' and hurried away.

The bare, little larger than a cubicle space was scrupulously clean . . . trust Sister Morrow for that . . . so Emma could go straight ahead with the heating and the placing of the hot water bottles under the blanket.

'I trust you intend to remove those before you insert the victim,' drawled Dr Harding from the doorway.

'Will you please remove yourself?' said Emma. 'You're not sterile.'

'I hope not!'

'I mean,' amended Emma, reddening, 'you're not aseptic.'

'My, my, what big words we're using today.'

Emma's reply, had she thought of one, was prevented

by the arrival of the anaesthetist from up the hill, and she went shyly after the three men to assist in the scrubbing-up. It was a very poor corner, barely room to turn round, and Emma, feeling superfluous, stood back until Mr Harding called warmly and encouragingly, 'Nurse!'

She hurried forward, rendering the services she had seen Theatre Sister render. The anaesthetist nodded to her in the same way as he would have nodded to a sister, but Wrong John said out of the side of his mouth, 'I can manage alone, pro.'

Pro! She supposed that was revenge for the 'fledgling doctor' she had flung at him.

She stepped aside. The men walked out. That familiar smell she had grown so used to in Southern Star, that sudden sharp pungency of ether overriding the ever-present odour of wax on brown linoleum, formaldehyde, iodine that had been her little world, a world she had left behind her when she came to EC, became her world again.

She heard the regular quiet assurance of the anaesthetist, the faint clink of instruments, the soft murmur of voices, and for a moment was back at the big hospital again, but there, alerting herself to the present, she would not be daydreaming like this. There would be sharp eyes to see her, she would be getting the bed ready for the returning patient, for Mr Harding had said it was not a grave matter, which would mean only a short operation, in which case the patient might be returned quite soon. She spun around and prepared things. She was just in time, a fact that did not escape Wrong John who wheeled the patient out, and, with the anaesthetist's help, put her back to bed.

'Just made it, didn't you, Blackie? Well, for that I hope she's sick.' He took up a kidney bowl and grinned devilishly at Emma. 'It's all yours, Nurse.'

He must have cast a bad spell, for poor Mrs Wilson *was* ill, violently so. For the next half hour Emma was on her toes.

During that time the other 'locals' were done and brought back. From beneath her bandages Mrs Reynolds sympathised, 'Giving you a run around, isn't she, Nurse? I can hear if I can't see.'

'I'm terribly sorry,' said Mrs Wilson contritely, out of the effect of the anaesthetic now. 'I wasn't like this when I had my appendix removed.'

'It's the way you inhale, dear,' said Mrs Reynolds knowledgeably. 'Now, with my gall op—'

Another spasm prevented an account of Mrs Reynolds' gall, and by the time Emma had coped Mrs Reynolds had forgotten about it, was released from her bandages, and, in spite of a bloodshot eye, getting ready to go home, and Sister Morrow had come upstairs to tell Emma to go back to Southern Star for a rest and not to report for duty for four hours.

'But, Sister, who will manage?'

'I should think I should be capable, Nurse.'

'I didn't mean that,' apologised Emma. 'I just wondered—'

'I know,' relented Sister, 'but intentionally and by design we are having an off day today. Only emergencies are being accepted, we've delayed the usual daily influx till tomorrow, so while you're resting I'll take over. And you must rest, Nurse, for you'll be sharing the Night with me. Yes, we're keeping Mrs Wilson here till the morning.'

'You mean—you mean I'm to—to—' Emma said breathlessly.

Sister looked sharply at her. 'Any objections?'

'Oh, no, Sister, I'm just thrilled to think I'm to take over.' She added, 'Thank you.'

'Thank Mr Harding,' said Sister dryly. 'He recommended it.'

'I expect he did that because he knew you wouldn't think of sparing yourself,' deduced Emma, a little let down.

'I rather gathered by the way he spoke that it was more of an award for you, Nurse. He'—Sister paused—'praised you.'

'Oh,' said Emma, and went down the hill to snatch her four hours' rest before she took over EC on feet that barely touched the ground.

When she returned at dusk the vestibule was empty. The only other time she had seen it empty like this was the night she had returned to relieve Sister so that she could look in on the dance. Dr Harding had been with her, she recalled, and for a while he had dropped his banter and spoken seriously. He had told her about Jason, his nephew, the little boy with the small white cataracts, the human reason he had come to EC.

Beside Mrs Wilson's cot there was another occupied crib—Malcolm. He was asleep, and in sleep once more he looked small, vulnerable and angelic, certainly not their menace. Sister looked at him, too, a moment, then, having learned the value of off duty, wasted no time in going up the hill. 'I'll relieve you at midnight, Nurse,' she called.

Emma thought when Sister had departed how quiet it was, how still. the rest of the patients, the 'locals,' gone home, Mrs Wilson, exhausted after her sick bout, no doubt feeling the effect of the anaesthetic and drifting in that after-ether, cloud cuckoo world, Malcolm sleeping the incomparable sleep of the young.

Without the bumping of shoulders every time you turned the hospital seemed quite big, if *he* was here now, Mr Harding, he need not sigh for the spaciousness of the new EC rising brick by brick each day. Going to the window, Emma looked out and was surprised at just how much it had risen since the last time she had spared a glance to the future Southern Star Eye Clinic. Why, at this rate of progress it should be ready to move into fairly soon. How pleased Mr Harding would be.

Scarcely had that thought come to her of Mr Harding's pleasure than she saw the great man, saw him quite distinctly standing at the new building as he had stood that other time with her.

Impulsively she leaned out to call to him, to say, 'It won't be long now,' or: 'Surveying your future domain,' because with Mr Harding, even though he was so great, you could talk like that—but something stopped her. Something in the droop of the usually erect shoulders. A futility that she had sensed briefly that last time. A sadness. A crumpling. Why was John Harding, *Right* John, sad? Was it—Kristin?

Mrs Wilson moaned a little, and Emma turned from the window. Quite soon there would be some pain for the lachrymal gland case, and she had her instructions. Pain, yet not too much pain, Sister had told Emma . . . not pain, thought Emma sharply, like that unmistakable pain down there by the new Clinic.

Harbouring a pain of her own because of him, because of her inability to help, even to comprehend, Emma turned from the window and from the unaware man leaning against the portal of the new hospital in a gesture of . . . *yes* . . . despair.

'Coming, dear,' she called to the patient.

When she came back to the window some time later Right John had gone.

CHAPTER ELEVEN

Mrs Wilson, the lachrymal gland case, had left by the time Emma pushed past the milling in-patients the following morning to sneak in by the back door.

In answer to Emma's inquiry for Mrs W., Sister Morrow snapped, 'She's gone up to Southern Star Convalescent. Only an idiot would remain down here by choice.' She looked balefully at the swelling waiting room, every seat in every bench filled, at the crowded corridors, at the street outside EC threatening by its overflow to need a fleet of police to create order. Yesterday's closed house as regarded consultations had had the result of an over-full house today.

'Only an idiot,' mourned Sister again, 'and I'm one. To think I left my quiet little observation ward up the hill for this! You can start with the seating, Nurse.'

Emma gave the crowd one look and quailed. It seemed that everyone in Sydney this bright morning had discovered an eye ailment and descended on EC. Two old faithfuls were with them once more—Alfred Croker and Malcolm. She must ask Sister, when Sister was in a more expansive mood, about Malcolm, how long they were to have him here, the date of his op, what would happen then. But immediately, on Sister's orders, she took control of Malcolm, and put him to watching over the drinks machine. Children were better occupied, she decided, though she still kept a watchful eye on him herself, aware that at any time the novelty of being beverage superintendent would wear off, and instead of going into the paper cup the brown liquid would squirt somewhere else. She was wrong, it still went into a cup, but when one of the front benchers complained suspiciously that the tea was odd, Emma investigated with a cup of her own. It was odd. It tasted of tea, coffee and cocoa.

'It is,' beamed Malcolm. 'You do it like this. Ouch!' For Emma was propelling him, by the ear, upstairs.

'You can ride around,' she ordered, 'on the ward trike.'

'No, I can't either, I can't see around.'

'No one can see around, silly little boy.'

'Around the side of my eye,' said Malcolm. 'I can't either.'

'Then don't go around, just go straight ahead.'

Malcolm did. Straight down the stairs again, banging the trike with each descent, straight out of the door, Emma frantically pursuing him, straight down the street. She caught up with him right at the busy junction of the next street, but he would not have been run over, for someone else had him. Mr Harding.

'Just as well I don't come by car,' the great man smiled. 'Back this way, young fellow.'

As Malcolm pedalled docilely in front of them, Emma said resentfully, 'He told me he couldn't see at the side, so I said to keep straight ahead, which he did, the villain.'

'Perhaps not so much a villain. He spoke the truth, Nurse. That's Malcolm's—and our—problem. He has that peculiarity of sight,' Mr Harding sighed.

'You—you mean that he actually—'

'I mean that actually Malcolm is suffering from an interference with the retractive media of the eye. Unhappily in his case both eyes.'

'Oh, the poor little boy!'

'Yes, the poor little boy.' For a few moments John

Harding walked by Emma's side without speaking. She glanced up at him and was surprised at the gravity of his face. Did that look mean that Malcolm—?

He must have become aware of her glance, for he came back to her again.

'Poor *all* children, poor *all* people with eye defects and eye worries,' he adjusted in a deliberately lighter strain, but she could see that the deliberation was an effort. 'I wouldn't worry too painfully about Malcolm, Nurse, I feel confident something can be done with him. Malcolm's inability to recognise the presence of objects once they are beyond a certain territory could either be a change in the vitreous chamber or an alteration in his lens system. In either case I'm very hopeful for him. Ah, here we are now. In-patients all set for a smooth inflow?'

'Yes, sir,' said Emma, and managed a wobbly smile back to the great man.

Wrong John, she perceived, as she ushered first Mrs Asher in, and then Mr Bolton, followed by young Chrissie Carter, was dealing with the objective sight testing this morning, his patients being asked to state what letters could be read on a test card. From Wrong John they went on to Right John, who measured the actual refraction by the opthalmoscope and any corneal astigmatism by the astimometer. How learned I'm becoming, Emma thought, impressed with herself. A few weeks ago I couldn't have pronounced these names, let alone comprehend them.

'Get cracking, Blackie,' hissed Wrong John impatiently, and Emma came reluctantly out of her smug cloud of self-sufficiency to attend to the flow again. But how different from Right John, she thought jealously, who would have looked up instead and insinuated gently, 'Nurse?'

Usually Alf Croker simply filled in time sitting on a

bench and talking with whoever would talk to him, perhaps win himself a cup of coffee from the drinks machine, join in a sandwich.

But this morning it was very patent that Alfred would not need anyone to prod him when his name was called so that he rose, smiled affably at everyone around him, then bumbled . . . *but not to the examination room* . . . out to the street. Instead Alf was alert on his own accord, and he undoubtedly intended to be attended. Indeed, he seemed quite urgent.

Wrong John took this urgent change of attitude quite well; like the rest of EC he had come to accept Alf and Alf's ways, but a few minutes later, holding a card in the usual manner over one eye for Alf to test read, he looked intently at the reading eye, or rather beneath the eye, then put down the card.

'What's this, Alfred?'

'That's what I've come about, Doc.'

'But you always come.'

'Yes, but today I'm stopping longer. It's this lump.'

'It certainly is a lump. How long have you had it, Alfred?'

'Reckon it could be some time.'

'Why didn't you have it looked at before this?'

'Because I could see over it,' said Alf, surprised.

'There are other aspects of health as well as ocular ones.'

'Come again, Doctor?'

'There are other—oh, it doesn't matter.' Wrong John glanced in the direction of Mr Harding, and, perceptive as he always was, the great man finished what he was doing and came across.

'It would never occur to him to attend Out-patients,' Wrong John grumbled as Mr Harding, at an indicative nod, looked at the lump.

'I'm here, ain't I?' pointed out Alf.

'Out-patients in the big hospital,' came back Wrong John, but he wasted his time. To Alf this, EC, *was* hospital, the only hospital.

'I'm here, ain't I?' he repeated.

'What Doctor is telling you,' said Mr Harding patiently, 'is that this is a *general matter*, Mr Croker.'

'What's that mean?'

'It means you're at the wrong place. We only do eyes.'

'That's why I'm here. This lump is no good for reading the paper—why, this morning I could only see with the other eye, unless you count seeing skin, and what I aimed to see was print. Can you fix me, Doc?'

Emma, who had held up the flow of patients at C, while Alfred was attended, heard the two Johns quietly exchanging opinions. Had she had any reason to feel pride in Wrong John she would have felt pride now, for he spoke confidently though humbly, and the older man listened attentively.

'I should say a fatty tumour, sir, probably there for some time yet unnoticed, but now drawing the patient's attention because instead of fluctuating in a small way it's fluctuating more freely.'

'I agree, Doctor,' said Right John, without any patronage, with full measure of respect, 'these lipomas fluctuate quite a lot. If our patient is patient undoubtedly his lipoma will recede again. That's the usual cycle of a lipoma.'

'It ain't me lip, it's me eye,' protested Alf. 'I can't read.'

He had such a sad face, and he was such a likeable character, in spite of his being their Old Man of the Sea, neither Right nor Wrong John attempted to suggest to him again that the lipoma would recede on its own accord if only he waited.

Mr Harding was looking at Dr Harding, and Emma saw Wrong John wet his lips.

'No use sending him up the hill,' he said, 'he just wouldn't go.'

'No,' agreed Right John. 'He is and always has been *our* Old Man of the Sea, and I doubt if he'll attach himself elsewhere.'

'EC, that's my hospital,' declared Alfred loyally.

'So,' said Wrong John, 'even though it's not our province—' He looked inquiringly at Right John.

'We do it,' concurred Mr Harding. He smiled at the younger man. 'Thank you, Doctor.'

Wrong John went such a bright pleased pink Emma nearly stepped forward to mop his brow, as Theatre Sisters did.

A moment later she was listening to Mr Harding telling her she soon would be entitled to do just that, mop a brow. *She* was to be Theatre Sister while Alfred's lipoma was un-encapsuled.

'It's a simple matter,' said Mr Harding.

'Me?—I mean I? I mean—'

Sister Morrow, who had bustled in to see what was holding up the inflow, said briskly, 'Take the patient upstairs and prepare him, Nurse.'

'Y-yes,' Emma stuttered, and led Alf away.

As Alfred got into the pyjamas that EC kept for emergency, Emma reminded him that all this should have been done in the hospital up the hill.

'What hospital?' said the stubborn old man, and Emma sighed.

'Why did you pick on us in the first place, Alfred?' she asked curiously.

'This is my hospital,' Alf stuck out.

As she busied herself with preparations, Emma knew she shouldn't scold him. Not only was it wrong for the patient, it was wrong of her not to appreciate a chance when it came, a chance she certainly would not have got elsewhere. Why, up there, she thought jubilantly, in *big* Southern Star, there would be an army of sisters to assist. No need for a doctor to attend to the anaesthetic, the anaesthetist would do that. Yes, she was fortunate to take such an important part in an operation, even though this one was not an involved affair. 'A simple matter,' Mr Harding had assured her.

But as she got things ready, the simple matter became quite an involved matter after all, though, sadly for Emma, one in which she did not feature, not even mop a brow.

Wrong John, preparing Alfred for his quick whiff, found a blockage in his throat.

'Something gluing up the works,' he said unprofessionally to the waiting specialist. He probed again, again, then looked up rather foolishly at Mr Harding. 'Sorry, sir, but I just can't—well—'

Mr Harding took over from the younger man, probed in his turn, probed again, then said, 'You're right, Doctor.' They both looked at Alfred. 'There appears to be something in your throat. Do you have difficulty in eating?'

'Not if there's something to wash it down,' Alf grinned.

'It is difficult when you don't drink?'

'Everything's difficult then,' said Alf sagely. He told them, 'You docs are at the wrong place. It's under me eye where I can't read, not down me throat.'

Wrong John started to explain to Alf that before what he had come to have attended could be attended this blockage would have to be cleared, but Mr Harding took advantage of Alf's mouth, opened plaintively to protest once more, to take up some forceps and put them quickly down.

There was a splutter, a gasp, then out came whatever had 'glued up the works.' A set of false teeth.

Right John, Wrong John, Emma and Alfred all stared at the teeth in amazement.

'But this is quite remarkable,' said Mr Harding.

'Very remarkable,' said Doctor Harding.

'They're not mine,' said Alf.

Emma looked round for Malcolm. Could little boys, could Malcolm . . . ? No, not even Malcolm could do that, could plant teeth down a throat.

'I had a bottom set once,' recalled Alfred, 'years and years ago. Funny thing, they disappeared, I never knew where.'

'Now,' said Mr Harding, 'you know.'

'Well, fancy that,' said Alfred, 'so that's where that set got to. And fancy me not feeling anything, though, as I said, if you take a nip at the same time—'

He did not finish his views on drinking while you ate, he said instead, 'Blimey, I can see again. See print, not skin. It must have been them teeth all along.'

Sure enough the lipoma had fluctuated once more, down again this time, and nothing could keep Alfred on the table to have it attended to surgically.

'Thank you,' he said. 'I knew I'd come to the right place. To think all the time it was only me old tats!'

'Mr Croker, this lipoma—'

'And you were right after all,' praised Alf. 'It wasn't under me eye that needed fixing, it was under me lip, just as you said, a lipoma, right? Blimey, I'm going straight out of this place and tell everyone I meet how it's the best hospital of all, how you two docs are right at the top. Reckon you won't be looking for customers any more.'

Looking for customers!

Mr Harding said it, Wrong John said it, Emma said it, as they all came downstaris again. The benches were filled, the corridors were crowded . . . Alf Croker could scarcely push out to the street.

'Well, we'll miss him,' said Emma, watching the old man leave the clinic, 'we'll miss our Old Man of the Sea.'

'A good miss,' snapped Sister, bustling along, 'and now get on with your inflow again, Nurse. Mr Harding and Dr Harding are waiting. By the way, you were extremely quick over that tumour. It was a very simple one, I presume, merely a shelling out.'

'No.'

'By simple, Nurse, I mean benign, nothing involved.'

'It was very involved,' Emma said.

'You *did* remove it?' asked Sister suspiciously.

'Well—no.'

'Well—no? What answer is that?'

'The right answer, Sister. Something was removed, only it wasn't what we thought.'

Sister gave Emma a hard look, then said, 'This is no time to be facetious. What *was* removed, Nurse?'

Emma called out ringingly, 'Davenport, Henry James, Deller, Muriel Ann. Will the bench please move up?'

To Sister she said, 'A bottom set of teeth.'

CHAPTER TWELVE

EMMA wondered if that flying glimpse she had had of Alf Croker pushing through the crowd into the street had been her final look, that EC in fact had lost its old nuisance, but she was not to find out the next morning, or indeed the next week, for she was sent on what Sister tartly called—Sister was being tart of late—'location.'

It wasn't anything so glamorous, of course, but it did afford a diversion, even though it took Emma for a period from EC—and from *Right* John Harding.

She was briefed that afternoon by Sister Morrow, a rather dubious as well as astringent Sister, not at all as sure as she would like to be, she sniffed, that Nurse could handle this assignment. Anyone would think, Emma inwardly fumed, that they had been Emma's teeth that had been pulled up by the forceps. (She knew Sister was still rankling over those teeth; so unprofessional, teeth down a throat.)

'What is the job, Sister Morrow?'

'We've been requested by PS—Preserve Sight—to contribute two of our staff to their oncoming drive. Naturally it will have to be our junior members.'

'You mean—' As though Emma didn't know what Sister meant, or rather whom.

'Yes, you and Dr Harding have been seconded to PS.'

'What for?' You didn't ask sisters reasons, but Emma, not at all pleased at this juncture at the prospect, did.

'Well, certainly not to extract teeth.'

'They were not extracted, Sister. Mr Harding pulled them up with the—'

'That will do, Nurse. If you've finished your day you can report to Dr Harding. On this assignment he will, of course, direct.'

'Direct me?' Emma asked indignantly, but she asked it of no one. Sister had swept off.

Because two years plus of hospital discipline had imbued Emma with unquestioning obedience, she obeyed without question at once. That is, outwardly. But her eyes must have disclosed what she thought inwardly, for Wrong John Harding grinned as she sought him out. He said, 'You look as though the teeth are coming out of your throat, not Alf's.' He added slyly, 'I forgot, though, if it was His Nibs performing the operation there would be no complaint, whatever the pain. What it is to be Right, not Wrong! OK, Blackie, you can skip the bow.'

'I had no intention of bowing.'

'I'm your boss.'

'You will be tomorrow, I'm informed, but that's still no call for obeisance. Why, Mr Harding—'

'I am Harding.'

'*Mr Harding*,' stuck out Emma stubbornly, 'is very superior to you again, yet he—'

'Rules with a surgery glove in which there is no iron hand,' said Wrong John. 'Well, no hand that you'd notice. All the same, I'd bet that he's not the soft touch you like to think he is . . . look at him with the rose.'

'Kristin?'

'That her name?' Wrong John did not pursue that subject, much as Emma would have liked him to, for she wanted very much to find out more about Kristin, and why, with Kristin, there was the firm, not soft, touch.

'This is our gen, Emma,' said Wrong John instead.

By this time they had left EC and had started the ascent to Southern Star. But for a moment Emma

paused, turned and looked back and along to the new
EC, its shell completed now, its thresholds formed, and
at one threshold had stood—Why? Why had Mr Harding stood despairing like that?

She stood herself, all at once oblivious of Wrong John
beside her, tears of sympathy, though she did not know
why, for Mr Harding.

Then, turning, she surprised Dr Harding's glance, and
the look he gave her was not taunting, not knowing all
and smirking over it, as she had come to expect, but
wistful.

'Why do you look back?' he asked in reproach. 'It's
not the beginning and the end.'

She stared at him in confusion, and he said, almost
roughly, 'There are other places of eye healing, and if
there's not—well, there will be.' A pause. Then: 'And
there are other healers.'

'But EC—but EC—why, you feel the same yourself,
you said so. You told me about your nephew and why
you didn't build bridges but took medicine instead.'

'All right, I did, but it didn't have to finish here, did it?
I mean, Blackie, there are other places, other territor-
ies. And'—another tight pause—'other men.'

'Other men than Mr Harding?' She was not aware of
the incredulity in her voice, the shocked censure.

But Wrong John Harding was. Under the Norfolk
pine thicket, to which, by this time, they had progressed,
he whirled her around to face him.

'Black—'

'Brown. The name is Brown.'

'Emma. Emma, why do you have to . . . I mean, I
know he is . . . I mean I'm the first to admit it, but—well,
I mean—'

'Just what do you mean, Dr Harding?'

'Wrong John Harding,' he corrected bitterly. 'Why

don't you call me to my face what you always call me in your heart? *Wrong John*.' He glowered down at her.

'Really,' endeavoured Emma, 'really, all this is in rather bad taste.'

'Since when has love been in bad taste?'

'Love?'

'Yes.' He was looking straight at her. 'Wrong John with Emma. Funny, isn't it?' Dr Harding started to laugh.

But Emma did not, could not, laugh.

'You—in love—with—' she echoed. But he cut her short.

'Oh, don't go getting any fancy ideas, it would have happened to any black-stockinged female under Sister Morrow's years. That's nature. But what isn't nature is you falling for him. Why, he's years older than you, and anyhow—'

'Anyhow?'

'You don't really mean even a passing thought to His Nibs—well, maybe a passing one. Ouch!' For Emma, stung, had reached up her hand and caught John a stinging blow across the cheek.

She had not meant to do so, and she stood appalled at herself, embarrassed; it was so—so corny.

'Sorry—' she mumbled, but the apology was never heard. For suddenly, abruptly, quite without warning she was in his arms, Wrong John's arms, and he was kissing her, kissing *her* (the only adjective that came to Emma's medically trained mind) unhygienically. At any rate the kissing was thorough, and have no doubt about that, silently sealed Wrong John's lips. Then just as suddenly he was releasing her and drawling, 'As I told you, Emma, *any* black-stockinged female below the age of Sister Morrow.'

'Thank you,' said Emma bleakly, 'for nothing.'

'In the morning, eight a.m.,' he tossed when they had reached the hospital. He added, 'I did have an idea of briefing you tonight on how to conduct a Snellen Card test, but—'

'Just as well then that you had a second thought. I've done a hard day's stint, and I wouldn't return to EC for you or Mr Snellen.'

'We weren't returning, Nurse, we were going to have a little lesson right here.'

'With all the staff not on duty looking on?'

'Not here. In my room.'

'Your room?'

But Emma's outrage was for nothing. With a little crooked grin Wrong John drawled, 'You would have been dead safe, child.'

He looked blandly down on her, and Emma felt an aching itch in her palm again, but restrained herself, remembering that it was undignified as well as corny to plant your hand fair across a hateful cheek. Instead she ran into the nurses' building.

Lorraine's, 'You're doing well, dear. Any more vacancies at the Eyesore?' did nothing for her temper.

And to think, she seethed, tomorrow I have to call him boss.

For all her indignation, though, Emma made an extra effort the next morning. She knew how important it was to look your best when you were dealing with the public. On street collection days it had been like going through the eye of a needle to pass Matron's eagle eye, and though on this occasion Matron would not be checking, Emma glossed herself up in a manner that Matron, and nearer home Sister Morrow, certainly would expect.

All the same she was totally unprepared for Dr Harding's reaction.

'Wow!' he said.

Annoyed, Emma retorted, 'Anyone would think I came to work like a ragbag.'

'You don't, Blackie, though sometimes your seams aren't straight.'

'How would you know?'

'How would you think? But today you must have marked them with a ruler, and you're fairly stiff with starch. Your hair, too, looks as though it's had a coat of paint.'

'I don't paint—I expect you mean tint—my hair.'

'That I'd believe. No such colour could be on any beautician's chart.'

Emma counted ten and restrained her itchy palm again, but had she looked at Wrong John she would have seen an entirely different expression from what she thought.

'Well,' he said, 'having inspected you and granted you a pass, we'll get moving. My car is in the quad.'

'Your car?'

'Did you think we'd go by bus?'

'I don't know what I thought, I wasn't informed very fully.'

'Whose fault was that? You were frightened to come to be briefed.'

'You never asked me to.'

'I did.'

'You said that you had had an idea of asking me but had changed your mind.'

'I changed it,' he stated, 'because you wouldn't have come. That slap told me that. Here's the car now.' He opened the door of a red Mini. 'Sorry I can't offer you something more lavish, Black, but in this instance any- way I beat His Nibs. *He* hasn't a car at all.'

Emma recalled that on the occasion she had run after Malcolm the specialist had been on foot. None the less it seemed unlikely that Mr Harding did not drive round, as befitted his status, in a luxury car.

She became aware that Wrong John was looking at her, no doubt trying, as usual, to follow her thoughts, so she said, 'Where do we go? What do we do? How long?'

'Our centre is set up in Parramatta—we're not doing Sydney, they can go to EC there—and naturally, seeing the drive is Preserve Sight, we try to do just that. I don't know our term yet.'

'How do we preserve sight?'

'We test, of course, just as lungs are tested in mobile clinics, and blood groups are taken during Health Weeks.' Wrong John halted for a traffic light and asked casually, 'What's your group, Black?'

'Don't know.'

The red changed to green and Wrong John spun forward rather fiercely. 'Don't know your group? You're not serious, of course.'

'It would be recorded when I became a pro, but I'm afraid—'

'And so you should be.'

'Should be what?'

'Afraid. Why, you little dope, at the next corner we could run into an accident and you could be bleeding to death. What would you say to that?'

'That you were a bad driver.'

Another light, and Wrong John stating, 'At times I could choke you with pleasure, but instead I'll stick the needle in deeper when I take your group before we open shop.'

'What?'

'I want to know your group, everyone should know their group.'

'Then I'll ask Records tonight, you're not going to go sticking needles into me.'

'As soon as we get to the mobile clinic, girl. Look, anything could happen—apart from my driving, which I can see on the tip of your horrible little tongue waiting to be uttered again. Why, there could be a fractious patient, a street riot—'

'Very improbable.'

'Lots of improbable things come true,' said Wrong John, 'and by that I don't mean Cinderella marrying a Prince.'

'What on earth are you talking about?'

'As though'—Wrong John negotiated a bend—'you don't know.'

When they reached the mobile clinic Emma saw that it was a chest mobile clinic made over again to meet the call for examinations on eyes.

'We won't open till I brief you,' said Dr Harding, 'because I believe we'll be rather busy, much busier than the chest division.'

'What makes you think that?'

'For some reason the thought of an eye examination does not alarm as a chest one does, in Chests people imagine all sorts of things, and, like the ostrich, prefer to hide their heads in the sand. But eyes are a different matter, they invariably think of sight as a matter of spectacles or no spectacles. Mostly,' John added, 'the female persuasion.'

'That's not true. It's a well-known fact that the male is now the sex most interested in appearance.'

'I won't argue that, I'm very interested in your appearance. Also that blood group. Your hand, please.'

'My—ow!' For John had withdrawn a drop of blood. 'You're a rotten injector,' Emma fumed.

'I told you what to expect,' he reminded her.

'I don't know why you had to do it straight away,' continued Emma, sucking her finger. 'You'll only have to wait tonight for Pathology to tell you the result, and that will mean no gain at all because I could just as well have done it myself.' She sucked again and muttered, 'You're a sadist, you did it unnecessarily hard, also unnecessarily unless you plan to double back now to find out the result.'

'I don't plan, I plan to find it out myself, in the little annexe we're provided with. Don't be too dopey, Black. These vans are equipped with the means to determine facts in a hurry. Good heavens, girl, an accident might occur in the street outside and valuable time be wasted bringing out a blood man. Now let me see . . . let me see . . . no . . . yes . . . yes . . . Well, what do you know, we're the same.'

'So what?'

'So we're compatible.'

'So what?' Emma glanced round the small clinic, from the eye chart to the big records book, from the table with the eye testing instruments in readiness to the darkened corner for closer examinations. This corner, of course, was well away from the window, but a glance through the window stiffened Emma.

'Do you know,' she gasped, 'we've already a queue?'

'I rather anticipated it,' said Wrong John, rather reluctantly discarding his blood discovery. He impelled Emma across to the Snellen chart hung on the wall, and briefed her rapidly.

'You've seen me do it at EC, and you've done it once yourself. It's quite simple, the distance for normal sight is shown above the letters, but in a small space like we've been allotted I suggest you save time and concentrate on that bottom row. On the other hand if there's obvious difficulty in reading that low a line, start a few lines above, and then see how it goes. The recording is simple, too.' He showed her.

There was also a card to be handed to each patient, a reading card. It started from diamond type and finished in pica.

'The records of names and addresses I needn't tell you,' said Wrong John, 'you're more experienced than I am there. Well, if you're ready, Black, I'll open shop. Oh, and Sister—'

'Sister?'

'Right here you're Sister,' he grinned. 'We thought it sounded more impressive.'

'In this cap?'

'Your starched crown, you mean.' He looked at her levelly, no hint of mirth. 'Queen Emma,' he said seriously.

A little uncomfortable, Emma checked again for that smirk of his. It was definitely not there.

'Zero hour,' he said, and opened the door.

There was no doubt about it that they were busy. Emma Snellen-tested eyes after eyes, holding the card over each orb as she had seen it done by John. She was rather pleased at the way she handled a volunteer immigrant patient, allotting him extra time to tell her the letter, to search out the English instead of his native tongue, when he still had difficulty to do this finding a suitable interpreter for him. The smaller children, too, she managed well, following their positions of the template, praising them extravagantly so that they were encouraged to keep up the good work. If any eye did not measure up to normal sight, she passed the patient on to Dr Harding. He was that today to her, he was not Wrong John . . . just as she was Sister to him, not Nurse. And Brown, certainly not Black.

It was amazing how many did have to be referred on for further tests, for eyelid probing for primary disturbances. Over a snatched coffee in between patients

Dr Harding said gloatingly, 'Five myopia, three hyper-metropia, two lovely incidents of incipient cataracts and one presbyopia.'

Emma, who knew by now that when doctors gloat over cases they mean as regards themselves and the experience they will gain and not the unfortunate patient, said of John's presbyopia, 'That's old age sight, isn't it?'

'Yes, and it can be helped. You treat it as a compound astigmatism and—'

But Emma was not heeding him. 'If presbyopia is old age sight what will this be?' She was indicating a patient in the queue outside yet unmistakably, by the way he stood a little apart from the rest, on his own. He was all of three feet, and all, she judged, of six.

'Certainly,' grinned John, 'not a presbyopia case. I wonder what the little beggar's queueing up for. He doesn't seem to belong to anyone.'

'Only,' indicated Emma, 'the dog.'

'Dog, is it? Glad you warned me.'

Emma looked at the pooch in the small boy's arms, and agreed, for it certainly was an odd dog. Instead of sloping dogwise from head to rear it veered quite steeply up, which set its bushy tail much higher than its ears, its nose, too, beginning aquiline like a collie's ended instead in the abrupt snub of the pug. Still, recalling her own childhood, to its master it would be what all canines should be, the one and only Dog.

The Preserve Sight staff grinned at each other, then started work again.

It was incredible to look back now and remember that last night she had dreaded this assignment, thought Emma, busily Snellen-carding again. For instance the poetic character now being probed by John was reciting in a beautiful resonant voice:

'Eyes,
Of microscopic power, that would discern
The population of a dewdrop.

                              Montgomery.'

'And that's what I prescribe,' said Dr Harding, 'dew-drops. You're a fortunate man, you've nothing really wrong, but you've let yourself go slack, that's quite apparent, with the result that the blood furnished to your eyes is not as pure and clear as it should be. So dimmed sight is the result. It makes sense, you know, digestion out of order, blood loaded with unassimilated material, then the sight grows dull and heavy. So fresh air—and dewdrops—for you.'

The poet bowed. 'The light of the body is the eyes. Matthew, 6, 22,' he agreed, and went out, though Emma would not have cared to take a stand on what brand of dew would be his choice.

The small boy with the dog was the next patient, and Emma sat him down and held the card over one eye. 'Read the second last and last rows, dear,' she invited.

Silence.

'The second last and last rows.'

Silence.

Oh, bother, she thought, another call for an inter-preter. Not that I mind, but it does slow the business down—either that or the kiddie needs the template, though I hardly think so at his development. And either that again or he doesn't even *see* the letters.

'The chart, dear,' she prompted. 'R.B.T.F.P. . . . the rest.'

'He can't,' said the small boy.

'You mean you can't.'

'I mean Bingo can't.'

'Bingo?' she echoed.

'Him. My dog.'

'But, dear—'

'It's him I've come about. This is an eye place, isn't it?'

'Yes, but—'

'Well, his eyes, one of 'em, is no good—look, you can see there's something wrong with it—so I fetched him along.' The little boy put the odd dog so near to Emma that she received a hot blast of doggy breath along with a lick of a rather rough tongue.

Surprised, she stepped back, and from that focus she could see that something certainly was wrong with the animal's left eye, in fact it was almost closed.

Her heart went out to the dumb thing so obviously in distress, and also to the dog's small master, even more distressed.

All the same she knew she couldn't help, nor could John, not with that formidable queue of patients outside waiting to be admitted and tested.

'Yes, there does seem something wrong,' she agreed, 'but wouldn't that be the job for an animal clinic?'

The little boy did not seem impressed. 'It says eyes outside,' he pointed out, 'and besides—'

'Besides?'

'Bingo don't know he's a dog.'

'Well, you could still take him and not tell him,' suggested Emma. Really, she mustn't spend any more time on this child. 'Look'—brightly—'I'll search in the pink pages and find you the nearest dog hospital.'

'You have to pay, and I haven't any money. You're free.' Before she could argue the small boy pointed out, 'It says so.' He waved his arm to the PS sign outside the clinic.

'Yes, that's true, but it's for people.'

'That's what Bingo thinks he is, people. He thinks he's my brother.'

'Look,' said Emma again, 'I'll ring an animal clinic and ask them as a special favour if they'll attend Bingo and we'll pay later . . . or'—an inspiration—'you could go to the Veterinary Section of the University. Do you know the University?'

'Yes.' The little boy had risen. 'I know it.' He took Bingo up in his arms and turned to the door.

'Have you the fare?' called Emma.

'Wouldn't be any good, dogs can't go in buses.'

'A taxi then. I'll pay for you.'

Emma went for her purse, then hesitated. He was such a small boy . . . the dog could leap out of his arms and run into the busy street . . . the child could run after him . . .

It was no use. She said, 'If you'll wait in there where we make the coffee perhaps we might find time . . . I'm not promising, mind you.'

'All right,' said the boy.

The afternoon's queue of patients was diminished one by one. The small boy, between Emma's ushering in, proffered jokes he thought would amuse her. 'You being an eye sister,' he explained.

Emma heard about the man who put a monocle in each eye and made a spectacle of himself and obligingly Ho-hoed. She repeated Ho-ho at a few more jokes in between testing and shoving biscuits that should have done for their afternoon tea into the dog's mouth to keep him quiet.

Eventually John came out and complained reproachfully that no coffee had come his way since lunch, and as Emma made no attempt to put this right, went into the refreshment corner himself, only to emerge with a slightly dazed expression.

'Something sort of licked me,' he said. 'If I didn't know it wasn't I'd say it was a dog.'

'It wasn't a dog, I mean it doesn't know it is.' Emma said to her patient, 'You're fine, something to be thankful about. Remember that on Doorknock Day for Preserve Sight.'

Before letting in the next patient she said uncertainly to John, 'I know I should have sent him away, but he's so small.'

'Not so small,' judged Dr Harding, pulling aside the curtain that concealed the corner where they could boil the water for their cuppas. 'I had a miniature pom when I was a kid and—'

'Not him, the boy. And I meant because of the traffic, you see the dog could run away and—'

'The boy? Oh, yes, the boy.' Now Dr Harding was regarding Bingo's brother.

'Myopia, hypermetropia, presbyopia, colour blindness or squint?' he inquired politely. 'Just take your choice.'

'It's Bingo,' said the little boy, and proffered the dog so that John got the blast of doggy breath and a lick.

'I thought it was a lick before,' said John feelingly.

He went and washed himself in the small sink, and Emma watched him dubiously. She had quite enjoyed today, in fact they had never been so amicable before, but she could hardly expect her luck—or Bingo's—to hold.

Then—'Well, son, bring that pooch over here and I'll have a look,' said John.

Emma crossed over, too. She watched John prise open the puffed, closed canine eye, watched him put in his opthalmoscope and peer into an appealing orb. Then, the opthalmoscope replaced, John began probing round the eye, the dog licking vigorously as he worked, his 'brother' sniffing back his tears, Emma standing ready to hand anything the doctor might need. Really, it was too ridiculous, and at any moment Dr Harding would say so, would object, 'Nurse Brown'—in his outrage he certainly would demote her—'this is not what we're here for. This is quite scandalous! Get rid of this child and this mongrel and—'

But—'Sister,' said John Harding, 'I think we can call it a day. Get rid of the rest of the queue, tell them to come tomorrow, and you and I will get to work on this seed.'

'Seed?'

'Yes, at first I feared it was a tick, but it isn't, it's a seed that's become embedded in the inner lid, and has actually started to grow, poor beast.'

'What will you need, Doctor?' Emma said as professionally as she would have had it been Mrs Wilson's lachrymal gland.

'Clinical spirit, tweezers, cottonwool, a light plug of ether to keep him quiet a moment and a good light. But dismiss the patients first.'

Emma did, quelling any dissatisfaction by saying that an urgent case had come up.

'Do you want to watch,' she asked the little boy, 'or would you sooner wait in the corner?'

'I'll watch. You see he's my brother, I mean he thinks he's my brother.' Bingo's brother or not, he was an intelligent little boy, he said in a worried voice, 'Does the doctor know he's eaten all those biscuits? He shouldn't, should he, before an operation?'

'And how do you know that?' asked Emma, laying out John's order.

'Tonsils,' said Bingo's brother.

It was all over before the little whiff of ether entirely lost its effect, the embedded grass seed was prised out, the eye washed and anointed, then a sleepy dog put into the boy's arms.

'Jings, thanks,' he beamed.

'Where do you live, son?' Washed himself, John Harding was now sitting back and drinking coffee.

When the boy told him he raised his brows and said, 'You mean you walked all that way?'

'Couldn't take him in the bus.'

'That means you'd have to walk back, and carrying Bingo, because by the look of your pooch he's not too steady on his feet.' John turned to Emma. 'Do you mind hanging on here, Sister, while I drive the kid home?'

He was nice . . . he was kind. Emma felt a lot of warm things towards him surging up in her, but all she could say was, 'I don't mind.'

She tidied up after he had gone, packed up the instruments, replaced the chart. Then she saw the paw marks and moistened a swab and got down on her knees to wash the floor.

'Nurse!' The voice startled her, so that instead of struggling to her feet Emma slipped further along the floor. From that position she looked up to the surprised and disapproving face of Mr Harding.

'Here,' he said at once, 'let me help you up.'

After he had done so he reprimanded gently, 'Never do that again, Nurse, never attempt to wash the floor. Good heavens, child, this isn't what you're here for.'

'It was today,' said Emma. 'You see I could hardly leave it like that for tomorrow's staff.'

'You are tomorrow's staff. You are here for three more days, after which—but what did you mean leaving it like that?'

'With paw marks, you see, sir. Bingo—'

'Bingo?'

'The dog. He came to be tested . . . I really mean—'

But Mr Harding had put Emma gently into a chair. 'Start from the beginning,' he smiled.

She smiled back, hoping he would take the same

attitude as Doctor Harding had, though she had little fear of any other attitude. Right John could not be anything but kind, she thought. And she was right, of course.

'That's good, I'm glad the poor beast was put out of his discomfort.'

'Then you don't mind?'

'Of course not.'

'And you don't mind us sending the rest of the last batch away and telling them to come instead tomorrow? I said that an urgent case had come up, which was a lie, but really a sort of white lie—'

'I'm sure it was,' he smiled.

As she had been babbling he had been looking through the records book, and when she finished he commended, 'This is quite excellent, Nurse. You and Doctor have been very busy. I'm sure PS will be pleased.'

'Well, I asked each patient to remember this service on Doorknock Day,' said Emma.

'They will be so pleased they will want you several more days . . . in fact that was mentioned before I saw what you have achieved. You don't look so elated now, Nurse. What is it? I thought you would like this sort of work.'

'Oh, I like it, but—'

'But?'

How could she say 'But you're not near, sir.' Then even as she thought it, the thought came to Emma that all day long it had not entered her mind, *his* absence hadn't; she had worked without even thinking of him once beside Wrong John. *Wrong* John? No, he hadn't been wrong today.

'Well,' said Mr Harding, 'even if you're not over-enthusiastic, and I dare to suggest that that's just loyalty to EC, Nurse, just worrying how we're coping, but believe me we are, there's something else offering at the end of the three days that I'm sure will appeal.'

'Sir?'

'You and Doctor have been assigned to spend a short time in the Interior. There has been an outbreak of sandy blight in an aboriginal settlement, and Preserve Sight feel you could be very useful there.'

'The Interior?' she queried.

'You could practically say the Centre. Where you'll be flying will be very near to the Heart.'

'Oh!' Emma said breathlessly. No Australian could contemplate the 'inside,' the 'Centre,' without that catch that she was feeling now, that sense of adventure, of *discovery*. Also, and Emma's lip twitched, Lorraine's nose would be right out of joint, not just another section. Not just another branch, another district, but two states away. Centralia.

'Well, Nurse?' He was smiling down at her, waiting for her response.

'It sounds very interesting,' said Emma inadequately. 'Thank you, sir.'

'That's my nurse!' He gave her some details of their briefing.

After he had gone Emma found herself forgetting the exciting news, only remembering what he had said. She saw again the kindly glance, heard the pleased, 'That's my nurse!'

Then—'That flaming kid lived miles past Timbuktoo, or it seemed like it.' Wrong John sounded rather like the ridiculous after the sublime, the abysmal after the lofty, as he burst in, hot, irritable, tindery.

'As for the wretched mong . . . well, you'll know all about it when you sit down in the seat. Next time you're tempted to play Good Samaritan to a pooch, put a muzzle on yourself before you make the offer.'

With that he slammed into the annexe to collect his gear. Not the time, deduced Emma, to break the news that a muzzled assistant could be an embarrassment to him when he partnered her next week.

She could hear in advance his disgusted 'Oh, no!' when he learned that their stint together was not yet done.

Well, two could have that feeling, *Wrong John.*

CHAPTER THIRTEEN

EMMA was sorry later that she had not informed Dr
Harding of the new plans. She had thought that Mr
Harding would tell him, as he had told her, but evidently
the great man had anticipated that Nurse, quite rapturously no doubt, would do the telling . . . though how
anyone could believe such a thing, thought Emma crossly, when they had only to look at the pair of them to see
how heartily they disliked each other . . . for he did not
seek out the younger doctor until the evening prior to
their departure.

They had finished with their final patient, and Emma
was tidying up the annexe for the next PS onslaught
under two different operators. She heard Doctor Harding say, 'Why, good evening, Mr Harding,' and Mr
Harding say, 'Well, Doctor, all prepared for the Interior?'

'The In—?'

'The Far West, the Red Heart, whatever you care to
call Willamagong.'

'Willa—?' began Dr Harding.

'Yes, it's a mouthful, isn't it? But youth has a vora-
cious appetite and I feel confident Willamagong won't
prove too big a bite for you young things.'

Emma heard Mr Harding moving around the mobile
clinic, asking questions about different cases; she heard
him commending Dr Harding on what had been
achieved in three days.

Then she heard him go, but was not so sorry she had
missed him as sorry for herself facing Wrong John's

146

wrath. She need not have quailed. Wrong John merely strolled to the annexe door and drawled, 'Thanks for putting me in my right grade, Blackie. By not telling me we had a further stint together you expressed very clearly that the matter was not even worth the mentioning to you. You are at least an honest woman.'

She stood looking back at him and wishing he was in the furious temper that she had anticipated; at least she could have understood that.

'Yes, I am honest,' she said childishly, 'not—not like you.'

At his superciliously raised brows, she reminded him, 'In love with me,' then could have bitten her tongue.

'Ah,' he pounced, 'so you remembered.' As she stood obviously reaching for suitably barbed words to fling back at him he got in first by reminding, 'Don't forget what I added to that declaration, that I would have felt the same for any black-stockinged female under Sister Morrow's years. In other words'—cuttingly—'choice, lack of.' A moment to let this sink in, then: 'Now brief me on tomorrow.'

'It will be more than tomorrow.' Emma added, 'Unfortunately.'

'That goes for me, too, but orders are orders. Where is this Willamagong?'

'You heard.'

'I did, but I didn't believe it. Surely we're not going out that far to hang up a Snellen test sheet?'

'There's been an occurrence of sandy blight in the aboriginal settlement, and Mr Harding and PS believe we—you can help.'

'We,' included Dr Harding magnanimously. 'A sister adds a certain touch.'

'Only I'm not a sister.'

'You are on these assignments.'

'Then that cuts me out of being that honest woman.'

'Oh, dry up,' he advised.

Together they gathered up their things.

'Plane leaves at ten,' advised Emma shortly, 'our car to the airport calls at Southern Star for us at nine.'

'Only a change of uniform needed?'

'I'm taking a dress.'

'Think we could go social, eh? Well, I will, too.'

'You'll look very nice in a dress,' said Emma blandly. He ignored her. 'Equipment?'

'There's a small base hospital at Willamagong with a district nurse in charge and a Flying Doctor calling. However, Mr Harding has arranged equipment we—*you* might need.'

'We . . . I know Mr Harding would do no such arranging without you as well in view. Thank you for finally putting me in the picture. I'll see you tomorrow.'

Dr Harding stamped out of the clinic to his car, remembered when he got there that she also travelled back, then sat expressionlessly waiting for her to join him.

Somehow all the boasting had gone out of Emma. Usually she rejoiced in announcing to Lorraine any new assignment, even one as far as the next street, yet here she was preparing for an extraordinarily long journey, a journey to the 'Inside,' and not even strolling languidly to the common-room door to drawl, 'Has anyone a fly veil they're not using?'

She packed a change of uniforms, jean and a frock-in-case, and that was that.

She went early to bed in preparation for the next day, but the flatness persisted, and instead of trying to quell her excitement so that she could sleep, as should have been the case, she found herself sifting the reason for the flatness until she was wider awake than ever. It was

being out of the orbit of Mr Harding for a further period
that was deflating her, she decided finally. Certainly . . .
and how had the thought even occurred to her? . . . it
was not the deterioration of the recent attitude between
Nurse Brown and Dr John.

For all her restlessness, however, she was up bright
and early, and no flatness could have persisted when the
air transport car pulled up at the hospital door and a
dozen nurses' heads—Lorraine's included—popped out
of the windows to see the departure. The Mail plane,
too, waiting to take off at Mascot, was not to be shrugged over. Suddenly excited, Emma got in beside John.

Probably he had flown before, but Emma had not, and
when the plane door had closed, the engines had whirred
and the craft had moved forward, then lifted, she experienced that initial soaring, never-to-be-repeated thrill of
one's first experience of wings.

Sydney became a Lilliputian city beneath them, the
postcard blue of the Blue Mountains reached up, then
the table lands rolled out, the plains, the black scar of the
lead and zinc city of Broken Hill, and then, thrillingly,
the first change.

Emma heard Wrong John Harding breathing more
quickly beside her, and knew that he was affected, too.
Comparatively few Australians had travelled into their
hinterland, but it was a goal, almost a house with golden
windows, Emma thought, remembering the childhood
story; it attracted, called . . .

The last yellow of the man-made arid region left them,
man-made because the mulga and eucalypts had been
eroded through overstocking, then the great salt pans
began, Lake Eyre, Lake Frome. After these came the
Arabian Night richness of the Simpson Desert, the
almost unbelievable reds, purples, blues and golds.

But long before this Wrong John Harding began to

talk, talk easily, pleasantly. To tell her about that small nephew again, his sister, his parents, he became not Wrong John but John, as he had been the last few days working beside him in the PS mobile clinic, and Emma found herself speaking easily, pleasantly back. She put it down to the comfortable seat, the whir of the engines, the relaxation, but somewhere within her, unexplained and unexplainable, she sensed it was something else.

They had to put down at Alice Springs and change to a smaller craft.

'It's a strange feeling,' said John to Emma, 'to know you're standing in the centre of the earth's oldest country. Do you feel as I do, not in the Land of Tomorrow, as we're pleased to think ourselves, but in the World of a Million Years Ago?'

Emma nodded, too filled to the brim to talk.

'That gap is Heavitree,' indicated the pilot, noticing their thrall, 'and the range is the McDonnell. Alice is a good town, it's a pity you're not going in.'

'We'll make it on the home run,' John assured him, and the pilot urged them to do that, then introduced the skipper of the smaller plane to take them to Willamagong.

They were not the only travellers. One man, an opal gouger, was getting off at Gibber, another, a cattleman, would be left at The Downs, and the third was a member of the roadmaking gang now laying out a track called the Gunbarrel Highway, nine hundred miles of sand, spinifex and mulga, to make the first-ever road to cross Central Australia from east to west.

'As well as the first, the loneliest,' he grinned. He would get off beyond Willamagong, which he knew well. 'It's the magnet around these parts.'

At Emma's inquiring look he said, 'Sister Drake, she's the only woman in more square miles than there's rights to be. Wait till the boys on the Gunbarrel know there's two dolls.'

'We won't be here long,' put in John, rather too hurriedly, Emma considered. 'We've come on a special assignment from PS, which stands for Preserve Sight just now in the cities.'

The roadmaker nodded gravely, the bantering gone. 'Reckon this is the country that needs eye education,' he agreed. 'Out there working on that dusty ribbon the heat fairly glitters right through your lids even when they're closed, then there's the dust to creep in and start inflammation, and of course every man carries his own cloud of flies. No need to wear a hat with that black shade to screen the light. Still, it's the land of the sunset plain extended, as Paterson said.' The roadmaker looked down on red sandstone changing from ochre to vermilion to shining gold, and he added, 'And the vision splendid.'

When the craft put down on a field of nothing at all, or so Emma thought, the roadmaker called, 'I'm sure to see you along the Gunbarrel before you leave, so I won't say goodbye but good luck.'

A jeep was drawn up on the nothing-at-all, and its driver got out and came across. Sister Drake was a study in tans, tan drill uniform, tanned skin, tan hair with sunbleached ends and twinkling tan-brown eyes.

'Welcome,' she greeted. 'Throw your things in and we'll get straight back to the hospital and leave any sightseeing for another day. I'm expecting a patient.'

Emma could not stop herself from echoing, 'Sight-seeing?' and glancing incredulously around her. She had been wrong about the nothing-at-all; there was saltbush, thistle, red sand, patches of rubble!

Sister Drake read her disbelief and smilingly said, 'I thought like that, too, when I first came. I'd love to show you now, but there's only Jimmy back at the base to settle the crowd when they arrive.'

'You said *a* patient,' reminded John.

'I did, but with that patient comes mother, father, brothers, sisters, uncles, aunts, and there they all stay until the pain is dismissed.'

'What is the case?' asked John professionally.

'A little out of your line,' Sister Drake grinned, 'and out of mine, I thought, when I first arrived here, but a few weeks soon put me right about that.'

'It is—?'

'An aching tooth.'

'I see.' John was grinning back at Sister. 'As well as Trained Nurse you're Dentist By Exam.'

'By Trial and Error more like it,' sighed Sister. 'Care to take it over, Doctor?'

'I came about eyes,' he reminded her.

'But wouldn't you like an infected molar down on your annals as well?' she dangled.

John could not resist the experience, but, and hatefully Emma thought, he included her.

'Sister Black always hankered after a spot of dental nursing,' he offered.

'Oh, good,' accepted Sister Drake promptly, 'I'll get along with the afternoon tea.' They had come to a low iron building whose roof glittered in the sun but whose interior, once they had stepped over the threshold, was delightfully cool.

'Change in there,' nodded Sister to Emma, and at Emma's surprised look, 'I afford every service to my native patients, even though it's only a molar I dress up. I rest the patient afterwards in bed, I allow his relatives to camp outside. Probably I might act differently in another base, but Willamagong . . . well, I'll tell you later.' For John, in full white, had come out of his room, and Emma hurried into hers to put on a white uniform, too.

But Emma, even had she hankered after dental ex-perience, was to gain little from Billy, the molar suffer-er, who awaited their attentions. The bad tooth was quite loose and almost could have come out with a piece of string. None the less, no doubt taking his lead from Sister Drake, John afforded him time and attention, put him afterwards to bed, assured his relatives that all was well, then came to where Sister Drake was presiding over a large pot of tea and a table of really surprising cakes.

'Ludy is a born cook,' nodded Sister as Emma gasped greedily at the size and variety of the sponges, 'yet for all her love of my kitchen and its many gadgets she's likely at any moment to turn it all down to go walkabout with Jimmy, her husband, and my wardsman, even forgo the angelica she simply can't keep her hands off for a witchetty grub instead.' Sister began to pour. 'By now you will have gathered that we're quite elemental here.'

'I thought there must be some reason for all that performance just now for an extraction and not a dif-ficult one at that,' John asked. 'What is it?'

'Not so long before I arrived here,' related Sister in a voice with the thrill and the wonder of it all still not quite under control, 'these very natives saw their first white men. We are still elemental, as I said. We still'—she paused—'have on occasion such things as bone-pointing. We have a witch doctor, too.'

'A witch doctor?' Emma could hardly believe it, not in her world, not in this age.

'Well, not here in Willamagong actually, but not far out. He's not the figure he used to be.' A flicker of triumph sparked in the tan-brown eyes. 'And that I put down to *my* way of doing things, Doctor.'

'You mean pomp and circumstance?'

'Yes, even for pulling a tooth. And I encourage the whole family to come along to feel just as pampered and important. I feel it would be a very rare person to prefer other treatment to mine.' She laughed.

'What sort of treatment?' asked Emma. 'I mean the other kind?'

'Tongues of lizards and legs of ants,' suggested John, 'dismembered rats boiled up with—'

'I see you've met before,' smiled Sister Drake.

'If you mean a witch doctor, only in books.'

'Well, the chapter you're about to open, Doctor, is real life and no fiction.' A serious look now. 'As you must be anticipating, our particular sandy blight that has brought you here is really a simple conjunctivitis . . . well, in the beginning, anyway . . . or a mere granulation, and as such I can handle it with lectures on cleanliness and applications of yellow oxide. After all, it's the sort of thing you have to expect out here with the sun, the sand and the flies. But—' A sigh.

'It's spreading,' read John. 'In several cases worsening to—trachoma?'

Sister Drake nodded. 'I suspected one granulation that came to me last week, so I turned the inside of the lid outwards and found the upper fornix covered with small lumps like grains of sago. I kept the man here . . . or tried to. He only stopped until news came to him that the witch doctor could cure him overnight, then off he went. I'm not worrying over him so much, he's only one, but I do worry over the spread of blight I see everywhere, because, as you know, Doctor, although climatic conditions can be conducive to eye troubles, lack of cleanliness, absence of ordinary hygiene spreading bacteria is a far more formidable agent. Besides'—Sister's sigh became almost a wail—'cleanliness, lack of, just doesn't stop at eyes, it begins a whole wretched gamut.'

John Harding was tapping the tips of his fingers together, pursing his lips in contemplation.

'Will they come to me or will I go to them?' he asked.

'I'm afraid in the case of the settlement that Mahomet must go to the mountain,' said Sister, 'though with our local boys it will be different, of course.' She glanced to the window, continuing, 'And a mountain it actually is, by our standards. It's beyond that group of rubble hills you can see distantly to the left.' She rose to pull the curtain further aside, and John and Emma followed her. To the left and west the hills rose, in the inevitable ochre, though even as they watched them they turned purple, then blue, then gold.

'What is this tribe, Sister?' asked John.

'The Pirintas. They move around a lot, but always come back here again. They are gentle, like all our Australian natives, and quite bright . . . look how quickly Ludy has caught on, even to sweeping under the mat if I don't pounce on her.' Sister had glanced back to the well-filled table. 'Then Jimmy is a really remarkable fellow when the tribe urge isn't on him, and thank goodness, for my sake, it's getting less on him every month.'

'You want me to treat the trachoma case?'

'I think you'll be too late for that,' said Sister bitterly. Then she brightened and added, 'Though at least when the others see the results of the witch doctor's "cure" it should make it easier for you, for as I said you're anything but dim. I'd like you to examine the inside of the lids of the worst of the blight instances in case of more trachoma, and then din into the rest of them what I've been trying to din . . . clean hands, clean nails, clean camps. Added to this, of course, the application of our old standby, yellow oxide.'

While she had been talking the sun had slipped at last behind the western horizon. It had taken a long time, a long golden time, but, typical of the Australian desert, the moment it disappeared it was night; no twilight here, it was more like a light suddenly being switched off. But the complete darkness was only brief, almost in moments the sky was lit with stars, great burning stars that you felt you might touch if you reached up.

'It's glorious,' Emma said softly.

Sister Drake nodded. 'It's a net and you get caught in it. I came here for six months and I've been here for six years. Now it looks like I'll be here for the rest of my life, because we both love it, and when the two of you feel the same . . .' At their looks of inquiry she smiled a little crookedly and nodded further to the north. 'Six-fifteen p.m., twice a week, from nor'-nor'-west to—well, you're not interested in particulars like that. Sufficient to say that that is Cal Renton, returning from his Wednesday "milk run", as he calls it, for failing an emergency call elsewhere Cal sees to the Downs area as regards their health twice a week.' As they looked they saw what seemed to be a large bird but was in fact an aeroplane passing through their range of sky.

'Cal Renton,' presented Sister again.

'He's one of the FDs from Cloncurry,' remembered John.

'Yes, Cal is a flying doctor.' A pause. '*My* flying doctor.'

'Yours, Sister Drake?' It was Emma speaking.

'Yes.' A little smile, a soft glow. How lovely, thought Emma, that rose flush through the golden tan. 'We started here together and we found we loved it together. And making that discovery, we made another discovery.' A soft silence. 'Well, so much for sentimental chit-chat. I'd better see how my molar is progressing, and what Ludy is planning for tea.' Sister Drake went out.

But long after she had gone Emma and John stood silently at the window, watching the desert's 'everlasting stars' blaze out to light up the extended plain, watching a moon emerge from a blanket of clouds and begin to soak up the remaining shadows that had escaped the star-beams.

John spoke first. He said almost experimentally, 'I once made the discovery of what I wanted out of life, I mean what I wanted to be. But I suppose it would be a small discovery to discovering—love. And that's how I'd like it, wouldn't you, Blackie—a *discovery*, not just falling into it as novelists write, then perish the thought of growing into it, but making the first discovery that it actually exists, that it's there, almost like discovering a fresh land. "Discovery" sounds new and unused and never known before, doesn't it, just like parts still . . . and can you imagine it? . . . of this big, untried, untrodden land.'

They looked out on the big, untried, untrodden land, they 'discovered' it . . . and for an odd moment in the magic of it Emma was sharply aware of a strange, unbidden, undreamed-of, quite incredulous—quite ridiculous—'discovery' of her own.

CHAPTER FOURTEEN

BUT in the morning the 'discovery' was forgotten, though even had it been recalled there would have been no time to give the incredulity of it all a second thought. From the moment Ludy called 'breakfast,' smiling so widely that John remarked with professional approval that she had a very clean mouth and throat and Barbara Drake replied feelingly that that was the only thing that came naturally clean with her, that the rest of the cleanliness had to be dinned in—'Oh, yes, I'm one for dinning'—it was apparent it was to be one of 'those' days.

'Bother,' said Sister Drake, 'I did have hopes of showing you around before you went out to the settlement, but now it looks like we're to have a clinic day, and even the Pirinta sandy blight will have to wait.'

Already seven 'locals'—Barbara called them that because they were permanent at Willamagong, were not attached to any tribe but to stations, homesteads, missions—were seated on the little verandah.

'There's no grapevine like the outback's,' admitted Sister. 'I haven't mentioned a word about you, but they smell out a visitor here.'

'Well, if it's eyes, that's what we've come for.'

'It will be,' prophesied Sister shrewdly. 'They'll complain about some small discomfort, then lead up to what's really the matter with them, something undoubtedly Cal is already attending to, but there's nothing of course like a second opinion.'

'Isn't that a patient's prerogative?' smiled John. 'Any-

158

way out here I reckon they deserve a change in doctors when they get the chance.' He glanced around him at the endless red vista.

Sister was right. Only two of the seven had really come about their eyes. The other five started off with some minor eye complaint, then brought in either their stomach ailment, their sore leg or their stiff shoulder.

'Yes, Doc'—the locals spoke well, no pidgin—'I am under the Flying Doctor for it, but I just thought I'd ask you, seeing you're here.'

John was very patient—and also very pleased, for both the Flying Doctor, Sister Drake, the patient and himself—that each time his and Cal Renton's diagnosis proved the same.

'Just what Doc said,' they echoed in satisfaction, as though they rather had doubted it, and ambled off—though heaven only knew, thought Emma, looking at the empty red dust plain, where they ambled to—leaving John the two legitimate eye cases.

One was a cyst, fortunately in an accessible position, so John removed it at once; the other was an early instance of strabismus, or squint, which obviously pleased the doctor very much, though he did have the grace only to show his satisfaction to Sister Drake and Emma.

'First convergent instance I've had, and a beauty.'

'You sound just like Cal does over an incipient something or other,' accused Barbara Drake.

'We're not as hardhearted as we appear,' assured John, 'it's the experience we're embracing. I'm particularly bucked in this instance because Emma here can cure it.'

'I?' asked Emma in surprise.

'It's a state, I feel sure of it, that can be checked by orthoptics, on which this lady is an expert, Sister Drake.'

'That's eye exercises, isn't it?' said Barbara. 'To the left, to the right, round and round.'

'Yes, but with some other movements and positions thrown in, the idea in this instance being to teach the sufferer to look straight out instead of down. You can have a session with the patient now, Emma, and later you can instruct Sister on the drill so that she can keep up the good work after we leave.'

The strabismus case was inclined to be contemptuous at first when Emma demonstrated the movements of the eye muscles, but when Sister Drake reminded him very pointedly how Dr Renton had cured a stiff wrist he had come about by making him exercise the wrist, he reckoned he'd give it a try. He was told to report each day they were there for Emma to direct him, then later to report weekly to Sister Drake. He was to go through the movements several times each day on his own account.

Feeling rather pleased with herself, and also feeling for the first time a little more reconciled to sitting in front of someone and performing what Malcolm had called 'mucky rot,' Emma watched the man also amble off.

Amble *where*?

She asked Sister, and Barbara said, 'All work and no play! Before you start the settlement crusade you simply must have a run around.'

She got out the jeep and they set off at once.

Emma supposed they must be following a track, though it seemed to her that the pattern across the red sand was only a wind whim, for the north-westerly wind blew strongly and continuously across the desert from November to March, and it left its mark on the vivid earth as well as on the bent vegetation. Barbara, reading her doubts, smiled and encouraged, 'Oh, yes, it's a legitimate track. Have no care I'll bring you back safe and sound.'

Feeling rather inadequate in the face of such calm assurance, Emma remarked on the wind bend of the stunted, bleached growth.

'Yes,' said Barbara, negotiating the four-wheel drive over a rather soft patch of sand, 'and there is something that might interest you two.' She waited until she had manoeuvred the jeep on to a firmer base, then waved an arm to a particularly bent patch of spinifex, some of it so wind-tangled that one would need to leap across or to skirt around it.

'When a man is on a bee hunt, and believe me honey is a highly prized commodity with the natives, he takes his woman with him to call out the lie of the land,' she related, 'because in country like this, inscrutable, camouflaging country, one can't take one's eye off the bee for one moment to watch one's step for fear the sight of it is lost. So the hunter depends on his female to shout out when to leap and when to swerve, and pity help her afterwards if she doesn't call in time. A patch like that diabolical tangle, for instance, could trip him up, at the least delay him, make him lose his focus, so a precious harvest would be denied.' At their murmurs of interest Barbara said, 'Now you can appreciate how very important are the eyes during a hunt, you can understand why sight out here is a very jealous thing.'

'How near does the woman run, Barbara?' asked Emma.

'She is his shadow.'

'And very suitable,' John judged, 'for woman is that.' When neither of the girls deigned to comment, he made a second comment of his own that it was nice to hear of a woman with her head down for a change, humility in the female being a desirable thing.

'Before I grovel desirably,' agreed Barbara, 'I have to see you two grovel first, for secretly you've been curling your lips up at the very idea of my showing you "the sights"—now admit it.'

John and Emma admitted it, and Barbara challenged, 'Well, *now* look around.'

They looked . . . and gasped. In the short time between the story of the hunter's helpmeet and Barbara's present challenge, a miracle had happened, a miracle of pink and blue and green.

'Yes, they are flowers,' smiled Sister Drake, 'our desert blossoms. Even after a few drops of rain a coloured carpet springs up, and when the rains really come the place is a floral riot. But I didn't bring you to a Chelsea show, I brought you to see—' Her last words were drowned in the changing of the gear control as the stout little jeep ploughed its way past two red sandhills, rather higher than the others they had rimmed.

At first, when Barbara stopped the jeep, John and Emma believed it was a mirage that confronted them, a shining green mirage with mirrored green trees.

Then Emma, fascinated, went to the edge of the mirage and dipped in her fingers and felt—cool water. Laughing delightedly, she touched the reflection, more cool water, but the substance of the reflection was not the expected eucalypt but a gracious palm. She looked around her. There were a hundred soaring palms, growing out of rocks, from the red ground, in ledges, spreading out their soft, fan-like fronds in exquisite delicacy.

'Five thousand years old,' said Barbara Drake.

They lay back under the palms, they trailed their fingers in the water, there was not a whisper in the vast stillness; the only noise to break the velvet silence was a soft trickle somewhere—and John saying quietly, 'I am five thousand years old.'

Emma shut her eyes, feeling part of creation itself, only emerging reluctantly to hear Barbara indicating the trees between the palms, bloodwood, beefwood, cork-wood. But her real reluctance came when Barbara said they must get moving.

'I'm flattered you like my backdrop,' admitted the Sister, 'but after all, seeing the Inside is not what you were sent for. I'll drive you out to the Pirintas now and come back later in the afternoon to collect you.' At their protests that this would be too much for her she re-minded them that she had a cyst case in the ward. 'Besides, it's FD day,' she smiled.

'Six-fifteen exactly?' teased John.

'That's the time of the Downs run. No, Cal will put down at five, so we'll both come out to the camp for you. It's lovely at that time of evening, all mauves and golds.'

As Barbara manoeuvred the jeep out of the palm glen again she briefed John on the way to go about a visit to the camp.

'Always ask for the Number One Man,' she instruc-ted, 'and never mention the women until they're men-tioned to you.'

'But their sight is equally important,' reminded John. 'They are necessary for the bee hunt, remember.'

'It will be mentioned,' promised Barbara with assur-ance. 'Here we are now.'

It seemed incredible to Emma that people could exist under such primitive conditions, but they did, and robustly, the children particularly thrived. 'Why, they're plump,' she said to John as Barbara drove off again.

John was having much more trouble conversing with the Pirintas than with Barbara's 'locals'. He and the Number One Man had to fumble their way between gesticulations, pidgin English and smiles, mostly smiles.

'They're a happy lot,' John said.

They were fortunate to have a sympathetic audience in the Number One Man. It seemed that the trachoma case had not got better and the witch doctor was not in high esteem. 'He doesn't actually say so,' John told Emma, 'but he's more than pleased to have us look them over.'

'Don't forget the women,' reminded Emma.

'They'll be included.' He looked at her slyly. 'Don't forget they signify the sweet things of life, the honey.'

On John's suggestion—and demonstration—the tribe were queued up and submitted to him for eye examination. The granulation epidemic had certainly attacked them badly; every eye examined that afternoon was red, inflamed, sensitive to light.

'But not,' John reported to Sister and to Doctor Cal Renton on the way back to the base hospital, 'intolerably so. Tomorrow Emma will start bathing, anointing and "dinning" cleanliness—thank you for that word, Sister—and I will proceed with the queue. Oh, yes, I think we'll break through.'

Ludy put candles on the table that night, smiling broadly, bringing Jimmy and the cyst case to the verandah to survey the scene, and afterwards the four of them sat on in candlelight looking out at the sky's candles, at the 'everlasting stars.'

'You know,' confided Cal Renton, 'before I joined the Flying Doctor Service I used to look at travel brochures advertising romantic nights on luxury cruises, all dark blue sea and big gold moons. I even tried it out.'

'You never told me that,' put in Barbara.

'I only tell you important things,' he smiled. He touched her hand and looked out on the plush night again. Emma felt one too many, and she wondered if John felt the same. But that would make two of them, and two comprised a pair.

'Come and I'll show you the Southern Cross,' John said a little abruptly to Emma.

'That's the beginning,' Barbara called laughingly behind them as they went.

But if it was, Emma did not know what it was the beginning of. John just stared up at the sky for a long time, said a little thickly, 'Now if Mr Harding was handling this case—' then turned without another word and went back to the house.

Puzzled, indignant, inexplicably let down but not knowing why, Emma went back as well.

The next day they started in earnest. John inspected, probed, turned back the lids of the worst cases to see if the granulation or conjunctivitis was something more than that, while Emma bathed, anointed, 'dinned,' and made disgusted noises whenever flies congregated on a baby's lids. She did it so often and so emphatically she felt sure some of it must reach its goal.

It was hard, but rewarding, work. By the time Barbara picked them up that evening, by herself this time, they were exhausted yet fulfilled. Much nearer in toil, thought Emma, than they had been in—well, in diversion, for that's all it had been when they had stood in the moonlight last night, just a diversion. And a diversion, she recalled, puzzled once again, that had ended almost as soon as it started, ended with John saying, 'Now if Mr Harding was handling this case—' then turning almost angrily on his heel and going back to the house.

Oddly it came to Emma: What case? The case of the Pirinta tribe and their conjunctivitis or the case of—Emma Brown? No, Black to Dr Harding. But she was being silly once again, it was the Pirintas, John—Wrong John despised her just as she despised Wrong John.

'Another day,' John was saying to Sister as they bumped back to the hospital, 'even half a day should finish us up.'

'I'll be sorry to lose you.'

'Rot, you have your FD.'

Sister, smiling, did not argue that.

John was wrong even about half a day, for he and Emma saw their final patient at ten o'clock. More gesticulations, more pidgin, more smiles were exchanged, then, each with a gift of carved wood, obviously the Pirintas' own weapon, for it was thicker and shorter than the usual nulla-nulla, or killing stick, they got into the jeep that because they would not be so long today John had driven to the settlement himself.

Emma, waving goodbye, did not notice until the Pirintas were barely discernible against the ochre landscape that John had not taken the usual track back.

'Don't be alarmed,' he reassured her. 'I wouldn't be foolish enough to strike off on my own, not out here, but Barbara told me if we had time to run a few miles along the new Gunbarrel Highway, which, incidentally, it's officially going to be called.'

'Is this it?' asked Emma dubiously, for highways to her meant concrete ribbons interspersed with concrete clover leaves.

'Look,' reproved John, following the dead straight track, 'this was done by five men, a bulldozer, a grader and a truck, done in gales, storms, sand and dust—what else do you ask?'

Emma could have asked for more civilisation, the straight bare road going into nothingness rather frightened her, then she was noticing something, it seemed like a flashing mirror.

'Look!' she indicated.

John stopped the jeep. 'It's a Very flare.'

'A Very flare? But why?'

John had started the jeep again. 'That's evidently what we're expected to find out.'

'But you're not going on?'

'I certainly am. That flare means something. I have a feeling'—John increased the speed—'it could mean us.'

'Then we won't be much use,' submitted Emma, who still wanted to turn back. 'You're not equipped, you never brought your bag of tricks today.' John always called his instruments case that, his bag of tricks.

John swore irritably, remembering too late that this morning they had only been finishing up a job, rounding it off as it were, not expecting a Very flash to summon them elsewhere. But perhaps it wasn't summoning them, he said, still extending the jeep, perhaps it was one of the roadmakers on the Gunbarrel flashing the other roadmakers on.

An unexpected bend in the road—a corkscrew round an emu's nest, they were told later, for no roadmaker has the heart to disturb a nesting mother—and they knew.

It was the doctor who had been flashed. 'Ordinarily,' said the man they had met on the plane from Alice, 'we would have driven to the base hospital to Sister Drake, but of all times the landrover is on the blink. It's Harry, Doc, he's run a three-quarter-inch mulga splinter into his shoulder, and it's down preety deep.'

John inspected the man, and bit his lip. It was exceedingly deep. 'I'll have to take him back, I'm afraid, I've no equipment with me.'

'You won't need it,' the sufferer assured him cheerfully. 'We've a good enough probe here, but none of the cowards will dig it in.' He gave his mates a contemptuous look.

As John still stood indecisive, he urged, 'Get on with it, Doc, it'll come out clean. This desert always does that for you—why, I've seen men wound themselves and rub on sand deliberately, and it's better the next day.'

'Perhaps, but that's not troubling me. It's the way the

sliver's positioned, also the depth it's dug in.'

'That's all right,' assured the man, 'I don't want to go back to the base with you. We've done two hundred and fifty miles of twenty-five-feet track this month, and if I drop out, and I know Sister Drake, the record will drop, too.'

'And your bonus,' said one of the men, and the patient admitted, 'Yes, that, too. Get on with it, Doc, it'll be jake.'

John looked at the probe provided and was told that it had been sterilised in readiness.

'There is a method,' he told Emma privately, 'called psychological anaesthesia, which consists of creating an irritation on another part of the body to distract the attention from the incision, which must be a painful one at that depth.'

'A sort of counter-irritant?'

'That's it,' awarded John. 'Now this is what I plan . . .'

Ten minutes afterwards the splinter was out with a minimum of fuss. Twenty minutes afterwards, having stayed on for a cup of tea, they were leaving the Gunbarrel behind them and returning to the base.

An hour afterwards it was dinner by candlelight again, for even though Cal was not there it was their last night together, then finally twelve hours later John and Emma were getting out of the local plane at Alice to change into the bigger Mail for home, their Preserve Sight crusade completed.

It was a disappointment not to run into Alice after all, but the heaviest dust pall the town had ever experienced had descended, and in parts the visibility was down to a few feet.

By some miracle the silent, sifting dust had not reached the airfield, so the Mail could take off—and did, leaving an eerie, orange glow behind it, and no one in Alice happy, so a fellow traveller told Emma, but the publicans. 'Dust-drowning,' he related, 'was the only activity being practised. Alice must be the only place in the world where the earth had met the sky.'

Reversing that order of city, mountain, zinc town, salt pans and desert, the big craft winged them home again, and—was it because of Alice and how Alice had let them down or was it just flatness after the excitement?—with every mile Emma became less confident, curiously deflated.

She had expected her heart to soar. EC again! Sister Morrow! Malcolm!—*Right John Harding!*

But instead all she experienced was an odd emptiness, an emptiness as empty as the desert she had left behind her. Though there at least there had been the everlasting stars, she thought. She stared out of her window now, saw a dull spatter and remarked equally as dully, 'It's started to rain.'

CHAPTER FIFTEEN

THOUGH anti-climax had arrived—for Emma, anyway—on the return journey, a further deflation, again as far as Emma was concerned, occurred when the duty roster, consulted, informed her that she had not to report for duty for another two days, that she was entitled, at least ordered, to take a rest period of forty-eight hours.

'It must have been all play and no work out in the Centre, Nurse,' Staff Sister commented a little acidly when Emma questioned her dolefully on the authenticity of the duty lists.

'On the contrary, we worked hard.' Emma opened her mouth to relate the orthoptics case, the queues at the settlement, the mulga splinter they had dealt with after they had followed the signal of the Very flare, but Sister, suddenly remembering to whom Nurse was rostered, nodded her authoritatively out of the office again. As Emma went she recalled her own dedicated days at EC with Mr Harding and how she, too, on days off had fretted to get back to work. That man, she thought, that wonderful man. Then she recalled Emma's extra woe-begone countenance, and hoped the absurd child wasn't getting any foolish notions. Undoubtedly, having once cherished such notions herself, she would have been unsurprised to have seen Emma sentimentally descending the hill towards the new EC, now almost completed, only awaiting its finishing touches.

It was late afternoon, and the workmen had gone. From the busy street that ran past old EC the noise of the traffic came muted and rather pleasant. The sun, barely set, flooded the new EC lines with a soft, mellow glow.

Emma sat on a trestle that had not yet been removed, and looked up at the building, *his* building, for she could not think of it as belonging to anyone else but Right John Harding. He had dreamed it, planned it, sown it, encouraged it, he had never stopped working for it. And, prompted a little memory, one night he had cried over it—well, not cried perhaps, men don't, and certainly never Mr Harding, but he did stand saddened and somehow lost. Had it been because it was not going as successfully as he had hoped? Had it been—Oh, why had he stood like that?

'A penny for them!' The dear familiar voice startled Emma, particularly when her thoughts had been on the speaker, and she jumped to her feet so hurriedly that she knocked over the trestle.

'You're in a rush to leave me, Nurse.' There was a gentle reproach in the kind eyes that Mr Harding turned on her.

'I was just getting up, sir.'

'Then don't. I mean can't we sit for a few minutes first, or'—a little wistfully—'after your week of the bush are you anxious to begin a round of city pleasure?'

'It was pleasure out there, and I'd love to sit a while.' Emma waited till he righted the trestle, then sat down. Mr Harding sat beside her.

'So you liked it?'

'It was fine, it was a discovery.'—Discovery? Why had she said that? 'I suppose,' Wrong John had told her, 'discovering what you want out of life would be small compared to discovering love.'

'Another penny,' smiled Right John.

'I was thinking.'

'I could tell that.' He smiled again.

Suddenly the thought of Wrong John irritated Emma; he was so young, so raw, so—

'Mr Harding, why do I have to wait two days to come back to EC?' Emma broke in. She really should have said, had she spoken the truth: 'To be back near you.'

He was looking ruefully down on her, shaking his silver-winged head. 'Oh, Nurse, Nurse, I told you before, never live for your work.'

'*You* do.'

'Yes, and now . . .'

It was on him again, that shadow, that strange despair she could not share, that she could not even understand. Then against her will Emma was remembering someone who obviously *did* understand, who knew things that she did not know.

'Kristin.' She was not aware until Mr Harding questioned her that she had said the name aloud.

'Nurse?'

'Dr Harding calls your—friend the rose, but I think her name is Kristin.' Emma spoke barely, she also spoke outrageously, for one simply did not speak so personally to a great specialist. But, characteristically, Mr Harding did not frown.

'Yes, she is Kristin.'

'She—she means a lot to you.' Just how outrageous could you get? Emma asked, appalled at herself but still unable to refrain.

'The staff on which to lean,' John Harding answered quietly at once. 'Have you read F. E. Benson, Nurse? "She was the staff on which he leaned."' He became quiet again.

But the sincerity of the few words almost smote Emma.

'I can't imagine *you* ever leaning,' she said.

'Can't you, Nurse?' His voice sounded a little odd, it came a little hoarse.

'You're so strong,' Emma rushed in, 'you're so—' She stopped. If there had to be a leaning staff, she was crying within her, why can't it be Emma Brown?

Then the crying was stopping, happiness flooding instead. For John Harding was saying in a different tone of voice, 'I never finished F. E. Benson, Nurse. After "the staff on which he leaned" comes "and the wings which gave him flight." I think, Nurse, *you* are the wings. Bright, young, lifting wings, like your bright, lifting hair.'

'And I give you flight?' Emma barely whispered it, she had never felt so happy . . . or so shy.

'I'm flying now,' he assured her, his eyes on the shining red-gold hair.

They walked back to the hospital again . . . but Emma knew she only thought she walked. Really she ran, ran with the wind, ran with sunrise, with birds singing, with a beautiful discovery . . . no, not 'discovery,' for somehow that word didn't belong here.

And, coincidentally, when she got back to the nurses' quarters, there was someone on the telephone for her, the coincidence being that it was the 'discovery' man himself, Wrong John.

'Hi, Blackie,' drawled Harding junior.

'Hi.'

'Like me, rostered off for forty-eight hours?'

'Yes.' Emma still whirled, still stood without touching ground.

'Then how about joining forces? I thought a run to the beach tomorrow, a swim—'

Silence.

'Well, Blackie? Yes or no?'

What had he been talking about? For the life of her

Emma could not have said, she only knew she wanted to keep soaring with those wings Right John had said she was to him. Wrong John was so—so earthbound.

'Yes or no?'

'No,' said Emma, not knowing to what 'No' was.

But evidently Wrong John knew.

'Thanks for nothing,' he told her, and rang off.

The third morning Emma reported back to duty, prepared to creep in by the rear entrance, but finding to her surprise that she could walk unhindered through the front door. No need to ask Sister what to do after she had finished with the seating, because there was no one to seat.

'And there won't be,' informed Sister Morrow, after she had greeted Emma, put her through a rapid-fire examination of what she had done in the Centre, how she had behaved herself. 'Since you've been away we've been petering off, Nurse, in preparation for our move at the end of the month—yes, new EC will be ready to move into that soon, so that now we are only accepting emergencies, operations, and—you might have guessed it—Alf.'

'Alfred?'

'Yes, Croker is back, and assuring us he won't let us down either in the new hospital. What we've done to deserve our Old Man of the Sea I don't know.'

'Could be he's our lucky mascot.'

'And could be he's our brook that goes on for ever, though I'm beginning to think Mr Harding's Kristin is that.'

'She—she comes often?'

'Always,' said Sister. 'Well, today is Operations, Nurse, and all fairly minor, even Malcolm's, though it does have a grave sound.'

'Interference with the retractive media of the eye,' remembered Emma, and Sister looked pleased.

'I'm glad you pay attention, Nurse. You can go up-stairs now and help there.'

Emma went, and found two lachrymal gland cases, several cysts, and a misbehaving eyelash awaiting, but she found no Malcolm. Knowing Malcolm, she began to look for the naughty little fellow, in the cupboard, under the beds, behind the bathroom door. There was no Malcolm.

As soon as she was able she left the patients and ran down to Sister.

'Malcolm's gone,' she reported.

Sister was not at all concerned. 'Don't be foolish, he's not even here.'

'But you said today was his operation.'

'It is, but the Home won't deliver him till the appointed hour. So much better for the lad, and for us, than having him here, especially when, being an institu-tion too, they can prepare him equally well.'

'Of course,' agreed Emma, then she stopped short. 'You said—a Home. You said—an Institution.'

'Yes, Nurse.'

'But Malcolm belongs to a family.'

'Not now, and in fact he never did.'

'It was a big family.' Emma spoke incredulously, reproachfully. Reproach for Malcolm.

'True, but Malcolm still did not belong to it.'

'Because—because of his retractive media?' Now Emma was angry for little Malcolm.

'Please let me finish, Nurse,' reproved Sister Morrow. Malcolm was attached but never belonged to the family. The mother brought her children to a second marriage and the father brought his, but neither of them were Malcolm's parents. It appears that the mother was left with Malcolm when her first husband died, but that Malcolm belonged to a first wife. In short, though they are a worthy enough family, they are also a big enough family without Malcolm. So Malcolm belongs to no one—at least he did.'

'You mean he belongs to someone now?'

'He is at present at this Home.'

'But you said he belonged, Sister.'

'And your ears are too sharp, Nurse. If I said it I shouldn't have. I mean—not yet.'

'Not yet?'

'It's not quite final. The papers are not through.'

'What do you mean, Sister?'

'Well, it looks as though I'll have to tell you,' sighed Sister Morrow, 'and if I don't the child undoubtedly will.'

'He knows?'

'Yes, and that is a mistake, I think, I can't help feeling that most of our juvenile trouble stems from confiding in the child too much. However, it was as they wanted it—'

'They?'

'To adopt a child, Nurse, there must be two of you. Otherwise—' For a brief moment there was a maternal look in Sister's face. 'Though,' she went on briskly, 'he really is a broth of a lad.'

'Sister, the *two*?' begged Emma.

'The other person beside Alfred who is always with us,' said Sister cryptically, busying herself on Records.

'Kristin?'

'It's very incorrect of you to speak of her by her name like that.'

'But you yourself said Mr Harding's Kristin,' reminded Emma. Also John Harding himself had said it, remembered her heart, he had said she was the staff on which he leaned.

'Well, I should have watched my tongue,' snapped
Sister. 'I gave you duties upstairs, Nurse, so please
attend to them.'

'Yes, Sister, but when it's a pair, as you said, haven't
they—haven't they to be married?'

'Most certainly, Nurse, as of course they are. Now do I
have to bid you again?'

'No, Sister, you don't.' Emma went up the stairs, but
with each step her heart went down.

He's married. He's married to the rose, to the thorn,
well, anyway he's married to Kristin. I knew all along
she meant something very precious to him, she was his
staff, he said so, but somehow I didn't mind, not when I
was his wings. What exactly did he say? his 'bright lifting
wings,' his 'wings for flight.' Oh, it's not fair, it's not
right, no one should say that when there—when there is
a wife.

Mr Harding was passing along the ward when she
reached the door, but he was not looking at her, not
looking and bidding like the last time, 'Penny for them?'
for undoubtedly he was absorbed with his own thoughts,
and, consumed though she was with her own misery,
Emma could not help seeing how very deep he was in
those thoughts. That she did not imagine it was evident
when Wrong John Harding, who evidently had climbed
the stairs ready for duty not far behind her, whispered in
Emma's ear, 'What's wrong with our great man, Black?
He looks a little distrait today.'

'Perhaps Malcolm's is a serious operation.' She said it
dubiously, she knew that his work never worried Right
John Harding.

'It's serious but not grave, he told me so last night. He
told me all about it when he told me how I was to assist
him with Malcolm, how I was to—Oh, hell!' Wrong
John was looking disgustedly behind him at two other

doctors now climbing the stairs.

'Who are they?' asked Emma.

'Pederson and Grantham. Eye men from City Districts Hospital. Why has he borrowed from CDH when he distinctly told me that I—'

But Wrong John never finished his grouch. At that moment Mr Harding turned and saw him—but, Emma realised dolefully, never saw her—and beckoned Wrong John across.

Together they walked into an ante-room.

One of the consulting doctors called, 'Nurse!' and instinctively Emma obeyed, thanking her years of unquestioning compliance for her automatic service now, for that's what it was, automatic. Her heart wasn't in it, it was in there, in the ante-room, with Right and Wrong John.

It seemed an age before the two men emerged again, and then a very strange thing happened. Neither of them went into the operating theatre, instead, side by side, they went downstairs.

The lachrymal gland was done. By the CDH men. The cysts were done. The difficult lash. Malcolm arrived from the Home that was minding him until his operation was over and his foster-parents claimed him, arrived sleepily compliant, and he, too, was done and put to bed.

The morning stretched into noon, the noon into afternoon and evening.

'You have worked well, Nurse,' said Sister Morrow falsely, for she must have known that Emma had *not*, had only moved and functioned mechanically . . . as Sister had herself.

'Sister—' began Emma.

'Not now, Nurse.'

'But, Sister—'

'No!'

'If I understood—'

'I don't understand myself . . . not completely . . . but I expect we all will, soon.'

'Tomorrow?' There was appeal now in Emma's voice, urgency.

'Perhaps. You may go now, Nurse.'

'I—I thought I'd stop on with Malcolm.'

'Malcolm has been returned to the Home hours ago, Nurse.' But there was no reproof in Sister's voice for Emma not noticing, for Sister was just as listless, and lost, herself.

'There is nothing to stay in EC for,' she went on in the same tired tone. 'In fact there will be no need for you to report tomorrow. I told you we'd been petering off prior to our moving. Well, I think this is the end of your duty here, Nurse. I'll ring Staff Sister after you go, and you must consult her. She will tell you where you are to resume again.'

'Yes, Sister.' But Emma still stood.

'You've been a good girl,' Sister said a little sharply. 'Don't spoil it now by questioning me when I can't answer. Go when you're told.'

'Yes, Sister.' Emma gave her a last appealing look, found no reply, and went.

Perhaps, she thought, as she climbed the hill, Wrong John will step out of the Norfolk pine thicket, explain it all, tell me what it was about. Perhaps—

He was not there. He was nowhere in sight. No one she could ask was in sight.

But Emma, through the hospital grapevine, soon learned on her own. She learned that Mr John Harding was in the surgical ward of Southern Star *as a patient* . . . that tomorrow there was to be an operation for a suspected tumour on the brain.

CHAPTER SIXTEEN

WHEN Lorraine said that night, 'This oh-so-important Mr Harding that everyone's catching their breath over, walking on tiptoe because of—why are they?' Emma had to hold on to herself not to cry out. And yet, she thought fairly, a short time ago *I* was the same, when I first went down to EC. I didn't know John Harding, except, vaguely, as a name.

She recalled other times when important people had been ill at Southern Star and how there had been the same sort of poignant hush that there was now, she remembered that like Lorraine she had been impressed yet not really touched.

It was different this time. Every moment of waiting was an agony, every door opening could mean a doctor or a sister with something good—or not good—to tell.

All Emma had learned was that Mr John Harding had undergone an exploratory examination . . . it would be at the same time that Malcolm was receiving his correction for the interference with the retractive media of his eye. (How had little Malcolm come out of that operation? Emma thought guiltily. I don't know because I never even inquired.) She had learned that following examination there had been sedation prior to surgery.

'They say,' reported Lorraine, who seemed to hear these things, 'that there is a definite abscess and it could mean a tumour, and that means—'

Emma cried to herself, 'Oh, no!'

She wished she could see Wrong John. He would tell her honestly, she knew that, because, for all his talk of

180

'His Nibs' and 'the Great Harding,' she was aware that John thought as deeply, if different, of the specialist as she did, and that truth was the only commodity he would deal in when it was to questions on *Mr* Harding that he replied.

'The operation,' went on Lorraine busily, 'is in the morning. There's going to be a traffic diversion to defeat the noise. Every medical big-shot will be there.'

Lorraine obviously was excited, and if it were not that she would have been the same as Lorraine had not all those things happened to her from that day when she first had walked disconsolately down to the Eyesore, Emma would have rushed outside.

As it was she escaped as soon as she could without attracting their notice, which was the length of time it took the girls to decide that even though Brownie did work down at EC she knew no more about the business than they did themselves, so lost interest in her.

Emma walked through the thicket, willing Wrong John to jump out on her as he had so often, but once more nothing happened. She walked on to the clinic.

EC was closed, something she had never seen before. Where will the emergencies go, she wondered, the accidents?

Then she read a notice on the door that eye casualties were to present themselves to Southern Star proper. Old Thane, the janitor, coming out at that moment, said, 'We put the notice up in case anyone still came along, but in the last week they've all been told that old EC is closing until the new clinic takes its place, so I don't expect anyone knocking on the door. How is Mr Harding, Nurse?'

Emma said as professionally as she could the usual as well as can be expected, which undoubtedly old Thane expected.

Then she asked him if he knew anything of Malcolm. She knew he had been returned to the home but she did not know which home. 'I don't want to worry Sister Morrow,' she added, 'by asking her.'

Fortunately Thane was interested as well as alert and could tell Emma that the little boy had been taken back to Thorpside, where he was being looked after until he went to his new family. 'Lucky boy,' said Thane, 'to go to people like that.'

'Yes,' agreed Emma, trying to swallow a lump in her throat.

There was plenty for her to do . . . for instance Staff Sister had already allotted her T and A tomorrow, the hated Tonsils and Adenoids, which entailed as well as adroitness with the kidney bowl a seemingly endless round of temperature taking, children being so up one minute and the next so down, and Emma, after weeks of 'seating' and 'eye exercising' and other un-wardlike duties, being a little out of practice and needing to refer to her Manual, but for all her possible shortcomings she decided to drop everything and instead go to Thorpside to see her small menace.

She knew the district where Thorpside was situated, so within a comparatively short while was walking up the drive of the attractive old home. Thorpside was not so much an orphanage as a child refuge. No children were kept long, which emphasised the authenticity, had Emma doubted it, of what Sister Morrow and Mr Thane had said, that Malcolm soon would belong to someone, that in the future his was to be a very different kind of home. Well, good luck to Malcolm . . . but Emma wished she could say it with more heart.

It did not help much when Matron allowed her to go to Malcolm's bedside to find that someone else was already there. The rose—or rather the thorn to Emma.

'Hullo,' said Emma rather uncomfortably. She could not call her Kristin, but on the other hand she simply could not bring herself to say Mrs Harding. And perhaps—perhaps she was *not* Mrs Harding . . .

'Why, Nurse Brown, this is good of you,' said Kristin. To Malcolm, eyes bound, she said, 'Guess who, darling?'

'You just said,' grunted Malcolm. 'That nurse.'

Emma sat on the other side of Malcolm, and as well as uncomfortable she began to feel indignant. For Mrs Harding looked—well, she looked replete. How could she look like that when up in the surgical ward in Southern Star—

'You know our good news?' asked Kristin.

'About Malcolm?' It would have to be that, surely, unless Mrs Harding hugged close to her a private reassurance of her husband's health.

'Of course. It's wonderful, isn't it?' Kristin took Malcolm's hand, and wonder of wonders the little boy did not grab his own hand away, make some disparaging remark like his favourite 'Mucky rot.' He just lay there happily relaxed.

After they had left the child and were walking down the Thorpside drive together, Emma was once more unsettled. Malcolm's trusting hand in Kristin's had disturbed her, it was so—so *right* there, but so, too, did Kristin's quiet confidence. This woman was—well, she was everything that Emma . . . jealously . . . did not want in Right John's wife. She was good, she was sweet, she obviously understood children perfectly and lovingly, Malcolm was indeed lucky, as Thane had said, for as well as having a father like—no, she could not bring herself to say his name—have a mother like Mr Harding's wife.

'I always wanted a family,' Kristin was telling Emma, 'and so did Jack.' Jack? No, not Right John Harding, that simply was not right. Never *Jack.*

'I love their small confused world of long legs and grown-up voices,' Kristin was continuing happily, 'the stairs that are a steep climb to them, their nights that start at half past six.' She laughed softly, and with maternal anticipation.

'Mrs—' blundered Emma.

'Harding . . . but why not Kristin, Emma? It is Emma, isn't it?'

'Yes.' A gulp. 'Mrs—er—Kristin, you seem—happy.'

'Oh, I am. Very, very happy. I wanted this.'

'You mean—Malcolm?'

'Everything, Nurse,' said Kristin Harding. 'I wanted everything as everything is turning out.' She repeated emphatically, 'Everything. I *prayed* for it like this.'

She pressed Emma's hand when she left.

Emma did not sleep that night, with the consequence that she was anything but bright on her first morning back at Southern Star . . . and T and A. Fortunately her slowness passed unnoticed, for her sister-in-charge was working with the eye not directed on weeping little T and A's directed on the operating theatre, for she, too, had once worked at EC and with Mr Harding.

When just before noon the news came that it was all over, and successfully over, the relief was so mutual that the sister-in-charge, instead of rebuking Emma when she smashed a bowl, smashed one herself.

'Does that mean that Right John—that Mr Harding is going to be all right?'

'You heard, Nurse, it was a successful operation.' Now that the tension was gone Sister intended wasting no more time and began finding out all the jobs that Emma had left undone.

But the longest day comes to an end, and this one did, and from the thicket, as though she had willed it, though she hadn't, she was too tired, stepped Wrong John.

Suddenly unable to stop herself, Emma flew to his arms. He held her tightly . . . *for exactly one second*.

For Emma sobbed, 'Mr Harding . . . Right John . . .' and was promptly released.

'I might have known,' Wrong John said.

He stood looking down on her, smoulderingly, reproachfully, but Emma only wanted to understand it all, not *see*.

'Tell me,' she begged.

'You must know yourself by this.'

'I know nothing except that John—that he had a brain tumour, and that that was the reason he—'

'He couldn't operate on Malcolm,' confirmed Wrong John.

'And the reason,' added Emma, 'he used to stand sadly at times, and somehow lost.'

'Yes,' agreed Wrong John, his smouldering temporarily douched, 'he's had this thing hanging over him for months. Being a medical man, he recognised the symptoms. He naturally put them down as we all would to a brain tumour, which would eventually result in blindness or death. To Harding it would have made no difference. The blindness to a man like him would have been death.'

'And was it what he feared?'

'No, the tumour was benign, this morning's operation removed it successfully, completely, and, as it happened, quite unnecessarily. It was nothing, which John Harding would have found out had he sought an opinion long before he did.'

'Why didn't he?'

'Because eyes are his life . . . *his only life*, Emma.' Wrong John's own eyes were on Emma . . . drivingly on her. But she did not heed.

'Because he wanted to hang on as long as he could,' Wrong John added, 'and hang on he did, until the morning of Malcolm's operation. He realised then the risk it could be, and called in the other men, decided at last to ask for an opinion on himself. I'—there was a little pride in Wrong John—'was the first to be told of his decision to do that, it was in the ante-room, he had called me over to him, remember? Then I was the one who went with him to learn the truth.'

'That it wasn't a tumour?'

'Don't be a nit, that sort of thing can't be told from a superficial examination. No, I was the one to be with him when he was told that only an operation could say in all certainty.'

'How—how did he take it?'

'As Harding would, of course, as any man would who has lived with such a thing for so long almost by himself.'

'Almost—' whispered Emma.

'Kristin, of course, knew.'

'Of course,' Emma agreed.

Another pair were entering the thicket. Automatically Emma and Wrong John moved forward together to emerge.

Casually Wrong John asked, 'What have they given you now, Blackie?'

'T and A—No need to laugh!' For Wrong John *was* laughing, indeed, he was splitting his sides.

'There is need,' he gurgled. 'I'm at the other end of the conveyor belt, I'm taking the T and A's out and passing them along to you. Well, good luck, kid, and many kidney bowls.' He grinned diabolically as he left.

A week went by. Emma did her work mechanically, she even did it passably well, but, as her T and A sister said, she could never be termed 'inspired.'

'Which rather surprised me,' Sister Leith commented astringently, 'when Staff Sister told me that Mr Harding had asked to see you.'

'See me?' echoed Emma.

'Surprises you, too,' nodded Sister. 'Well, run along, child.'

'Where?'

'To his room, of course. He's up, but still resting. The weeks that led to what happened have taken their toll, and he's having a well-earned break.'

'How—how long can I stop?'

'Don't worry,' said Sister nastily, 'he's a born medical man, he'll throw you out.'

Which, in a way, John Harding did.

After Emma had knocked shyly and gone in, John Harding had said, 'Ah, my wings for flight. Sit down, Nurse.'

Then, Emma sitting beside him, he had made a charming little speech about the way she had helped him.

'You know the story now, Nurse, how I feared the worst. In doing what I did I went against the very thing doctors fight for, they fight for and *implore* the patient not to waste time, to come early. Well, I didn't, and I was lucky, more lucky than I deserve.'

'You did it because you wanted to serve as long as you could, sir.'

'Yes.' He smiled. 'And you, my wings, helped me, so in a way you were an accomplice in crime.' He smiled again. 'But enough of this. I just wanted to thank you—and particularly, perhaps, for having red hair.'

'Red hair?'

'It was my light, my spark, it kept me going. Where everything was dark, and looked, for me, like being darker, you stood out in light. In hope. In what, please

God, might be. So thank you again for having red hair, my dear.'

'It's funny.' Emma was saying it a little hysterically had Mr Harding only heard.

'Yes, I suppose it all does sound rather funny now, he agreed, 'but not then.'

'I didn't mean that,' said Emma. 'I meant you wanting red hair when your wife has black.'

'Has she?' He looked surprised.

'Very black.'

'My wife has?'

'Yes, sir.'

'You are sure?' A little twitch to his lips, but Emma did not see it.

'Of course I'm sure, she's very brunette.'

'But I have no wife,' Right John Harding said.

Over coffee—for suddenly and enlighteningly Mr Harding had seen there was urgent need for coffee and the talk that could go with it—John Harding repeated, 'I have no wife, Nurse Brown.'

'But Kristin—'

'Is my sister-in-law.'

'Then—then you're not to be Malcolm's father?'

'Only his uncle, Nurse.'

'But Kristin was always very near you.'

'She is near me, as near indeed as my blood sister could ever be.'

'But—*Jack*,' Emma recalled, puzzled.

'Is really Bernard. He's a twin to that sister of mine without the in-law, christened Jill, with the not surprising result that as children the pair of them were known as Jack and Jill, and it stuck. Luckily I was always John, otherwise there could have been confusion. Yes, I love

Kristin, who took the sisterly place of Jill when Jill left to live in England, as I love my brother Jack . . . Jack, who has been worrying for months for me to have attention, and who passed his worry . . . and undoubtedly an order to do something about that worry, for Kristin has not let up on me for weeks . . . to his wife. Oh, yes, I love Kristin indeed. In fact'—jokingly—'had Jack not got in first—'

'You would have married her?'

'No, Nurse.' The joke was finished now.

There was a silence, a rather careful, cautious silence.

'I would not have married her,' Right John Harding said, carefully, cautiously.

Emma waited . . . waited for the quickened heart-beat, the returning hope, the thrall. But even before Right John said gently, tentatively, stepping feelingly for fear he trod on a dream, 'I would not, and will not be marrying,' she knew that what she had thought was in her all this time was not there at all.

'Eyes are my life, Nurse,' Mr Harding was saying. 'I know it's not for me to say they always will be, but now, freed again, given another wonderful lease, I feel that I'm sure.' He leaned across and touched Emma's hand, touched it gently. 'I think someone else is sure,' he insinuated.

'Of what, sir?'

'*You* ask that of me?' he teased gently. Then he said, 'I'm a little tired now, Nurse. Thank you for coming. And thank you most of all for those wings of bright hair.' He sat back, and Emma saw he *was* tired, the worry and the uncertainty had left their toll. But for all that he said as she opened the door to go out, 'If I were you I would take the thicket path.'

Perhaps he wanted to come to the window to see the red hair that had kept him going, or so he had said, these last weeks—well, it wouldn't hurt her to go back that way.

So Emma went. And with every step she grew up a little. She grew from an impressionable mid-way to a sensible level-headed, sober-minded—

'Em!'

It was Wrong John. In the thicket. And instead of her rushing to him as she had the last time, he was rushing to her.

'I'm to second Mr Harding in the new EC. He told me today. I wanted you to be the first to hear.'

'I've just been to see him. John, did you know that Kristin was not his wife?'

'Of course.'

'You never told me.'

'You never asked.'

'But you, and everyone else, let me gather the impression that he was married.'

'He was, and is, to his work.'

Now Wrong John was looking at her levelly, with estimation.

'Bit of a blow, isn't it, after finding he's eligible after all to be told he's not. For that's what you've just learned, haven't you? I can see it in your eyes. In which case I won't hurry you up yet, I'll let the pain ease off.'

The pain? But it wasn't pain at all, it was just something she had not known, but now she did. But there was something still she didn't know. It was that 'hurry' he had used. She did not understand what he meant, so she asked.

'What do you mean hurry me?'

'To be my girl. Because you are, you know. I knew that the first minute I clapped eyes on those black legs of yours.'

'Anything under Sister Morrow's years,' she reminded him bitterly.

'That was defensive talk,' he answered. 'I had to defend a heart.'

'Then there was the Centre,' he went on, 'and "discovering" love existed, that love *was*. Oh, yes, I knew, and I know, all right, but don't worry, little one, I'll give you time.'

She was staring at him, staring amazed, and yet not really amazed. *Knowing. As he knew.*

'How much time?' she said tautly; she felt suddenly strung tight.

'How long do you want?' he came back.

'I—I think this long,' said Emma, stepping forward, 'should be long enough.' There can be no pride, she thought, in love, and this—she knew suddenly and clearly—is that. She only hoped her coming halfway to him would be enough.

But it was not.

'It's too quick,' he judged cautiously. 'It's too nicely wrapped up. I could almost call it—rebound.'

'But it's not,' said Emma, 'it's not.'

As he still stood looking at her, disbelieving, a little suspicious, wanting to meet her but listening to that cautious heart, Emma said eagerly, 'I was silly, and young, and moonstruck, I liked silver strands to hair, not pieces falling over eyes, I liked Mr and not Doctor, I liked—liked—' She paused, then went on, 'But for all that—'

'I'm listening, Emma.' His voice all at once had a sharp, warning note.

'For all that I think in my heart, even though Wrong John was my name for you, that you—that you never were. Wrong, I mean. Instead—'

'I'm listening, Emma.'

'Instead you were Right.' There, Dr Harding. It was out.

But still he stood unconvinced, that rebound suspicion still lurking in his eyes. It all sounded too soon, too glib, too nicely wrapped up as he had said, and Emma knew she must tell him something else.

'I made, it, too, out there.' She didn't stammer now, she spoke gladly, surely. 'The "discovery," John. I, too, "discovered" love. That love existed. That love *was*. It was like that for me as well. It—'

But she never finished her declaration, or if she did it wasn't heard.

Not in his folding arms.